She was ready when someone yanked the front door open. Or thought she was.

The naked chest took her by surprise. Mostly because it was so damned big and broad. It was also roped with muscles and topped by shoulders that blocked any view of the interior of the house.

"Yeah?"

The bad-tempered growl wrenched Andi's gaze upward. She had one startled second to take in the instantly recognizable face—the cheeks and chin stubbled with dark whiskers, the electric blue eyes—before those eyes went wide.

"Well, damn!"

An arm whipped around her waist. A swift tug toppled her into that acre or so of bare chest. And the mouth that came down on hers was hard and achingly familiar.

‡‡‡
Mothers Day
Rachel Lee Vines
5/13–14/2001

Merline Lovelace

After twenty-three years in the United States Air Force, pulling tours in Vietnam, at the Pentagon and at bases all over the world, Merline Lovelace decided to try her hand at writing. She now has more than sixty-five published novels and over nine million copies of her works in print.

Merline and her own handsome hero live in Oklahoma. When she's not glued to her keyboard, she loves traveling to exotic locations, chasing little white balls around the golf course and enjoying long, lazy dinners with family and friends.

THE Next Novel™

Merline Lovelace

eX MARKS
THE SPOT

EX MARKS THE SPOT

copyright © 2007 by Merline Lovelace

isbn-13:978-0-373-88131-4

isbn-10:   0-373-88131-2

TheNextNovel.com

 HARLEQUIN®

PRINTED IN U.S.A.

From the Author

Dear Reader,

I love going back to my USAF roots. In *Ex Marks the Spot*, I revisited one of the bases in the northwest Florida panhandle where I rubbed elbows with tough, macho Special Ops types and dodged alligators on the golf course.

I also got to ride along with the book's heroine as her life took some wild, roller-coaster dips and turns. Like her, I discovered there really is life after the Air Force. And what a life it is! Hope you, too, enjoy the ride....

All my best,

Merline

To my sweetie, my hero, my husband.
We've marched lockstep for thirty-plus years,
making the most of every left flank or right oblique.
Thanks for the memories, my darling.

sister had grown up at bases all over the world. Carol had rebelled against constant moves and being forced to leave friends behind, but Andi had thrived on their family's gypsy life. She'd joined the Air Force herself right out of college and loved every minute of her military career. Well, almost every minute. She could have done without that tour in Iraq.

Her mouth grim, she fingered the tiny scar on the right side of her chin. She'd been all the way across the square when the IED went off. The explosion had knocked her flat and detonated an accompanying burst of shock and adrenaline. She hadn't even felt the shrapnel slice into her chin. Lunging to her feet, Andi had raced across the square to take charge of rescue-and-recovery efforts.

Sometime during those chaotic hours she'd managed to pick up a desert-borne bacterium that stumped the docs and proved irritatingly resistant to antibiotics. Andi didn't realize she'd been infected until almost six months after she'd rotated back to the States and a high-stress job with the Joint Chiefs of Staff. By then the bug had burrowed into her heart muscle. Next thing Andi knew, she'd been evaluated by a medical board and landed on the Temporary Disability Retirement list.

Except she didn't *feel* disabled, temporary or otherwise. So she had to pace herself, have regular blood tests and echocardiograms? So she was taking a regular cocktail of antibiotics? Big deal.

The eval board had indicated she could apply to return to active duty in a year or so, assuming she beat the bug. The trick was figuring out what the heck to do with herself in the meantime. Without the regimen that had shaped her life, she felt lost, cut adrift, alone.

Disgusted, she shook her head. Okay! All right! Cut the self-pity, Armstrong. Focus on the suspicious activities next door.

Andi knew the signs of a crack house. She should. She'd dragged her sister out of enough of them during those awful years of Carol's worst anger and rebellion. Thank God her teenaged sister had finally hit bottom, gotten professional help and kicked her habit.

Despite its prime beachfront location, the house next door fit all the criteria. The late-night comings and goings. The shuttered windows. The untended yard. The half-constructed deck at the side of the house—as if its owner had been juiced up and eager to start the project but crashed before finishing it.

Common sense said Andi should call the sheriff's office, report her suspicions and wait for them to investigate. Grim experience told her she needed more than vague suspicion to precipitate action. She needed an up-close-and-personal look at what was going on inside the house.

She had an excuse ready, assuming she needed one: she'd just arrived, didn't know how to turn on the hot-water heater, saw the lights in her neighbor's window and decided to ask for help.

Abandoning her observation post, she shoved her feet into the flip-flops she'd kicked off earlier and headed for the stairs. A detour through the garage retrieved a lethal little collapsible baton from the side pocket of her cherry-red Tahoe. Tucking the weapon into the back pocket of her jeans, Andi slipped out the garage door.

The humid night slapped her in the face the moment she stepped outside. So much for the cooling ocean breezes the Realtor claimed blew in off the Gulf of Mexico! He'd also neglected to mention the mosquitoes. Andi had forgotten how big and ornery they grew in these parts.

Swatting at a particularly vicious kamikaze dive-bomber, she crunched across the crushed-shell driveway separating her yard from her neighbor's. When she gained the front stoop, she leaned on the doorbell until an irritated bellow sounded from inside.

"Okay, okay! I'm coming."

That was followed by a crash and a curse. Slipping the baton out of her back pocket, Andi palmed it in her right hand. She was ready when someone yanked the front door open. Or thought she was.

The naked chest took her by surprise. Mostly because it was so damned big and broad. It was also roped with muscles and topped by shoulders that blocked any view of the interior of the house.

"Yeah?"

The bad-tempered growl wrenched Andi's gaze upward. She had one startled second to take in the instantly recognizable face—the cheeks and chin stubbled with dark whiskers, the nose flattened at the bridge, the electric-blue eyes—before those eyes went wide.

"Well, damn!"

An arm whipped around her waist. A swift tug toppled her into that acre or so of bare chest. The mouth that came down on hers was hard and hot and achingly familiar.

Time seemed to reverse itself. For a crazy instant Andi was back in New Mexico, wrapped in a dark sky ablaze with millions of stars, flattened against Dave Armstrong's chest.

They'd been so hungry for each other that night, so damned greedy. They'd left the Kirtland AFB Officers' Club in a haze of desire and had been popping the buttons on each other's dress uniforms before they'd screeched into the parking lot of Dave's apartment complex.

Another hard kiss returned her to the present. Dave

didn't release her. If anything, his hold tightened as he buried his face in her hair.

"Lord, I needed you to show up on my doorstep tonight."

"Dave!" Wiggling, she managed to wedge her arms against his chest. "I can't breathe."

His head lifted, and one corner of his mouth tipped into the lazy grin that had melted Andi's bones more times than she cared to remember.

"Just the way I like my women," he drawled, his eyes glinting. "Breathless and eager."

"How about breathless and ribless?" she gasped.

"Sorry."

Still grinning, he eased his hold. While Andi gulped in air, he curled a knuckle under her chin. His expression turned serious as he tipped her face to the light spilling over his shoulders.

"I heard about the medical evaluation board. That sucks, babe."

"Yeah, well, you know how it goes."

"Come on in." Looping his arm over her shoulders, he propelled her into the foyer. "We'll kick my team out and talk about it."

Understanding dawned. Those shadowy figures Andi had spotted slipping in and out of the house were members of his Special Ops unit. And the black bags she'd mistaken for garbage sacks contained Dave's gear. The bags were stacked here in the front hall, enough for a one-man army. Judging by that pile and the bristles on his cheeks and chin, he'd just returned from a mission. The weeds in the front yard and the windows she belatedly realized were boarded against the hurricanes that battered the gulf suggested his mission had lasted several months.

The old hurts came crashing back. Andi had gone down this road once before with Dave. She couldn't do it again. Especially not now.

"I didn't just show up on your doorstep," she said, shrugging out of his hold. "And I'm not looking for a shoulder to cry on."

He hooked his hands on his hips above the waistband of his low-riding jeans. "Then what?"

"I've rented the house next door. Trust me," she added when his brows soared, "I had *no* idea you lived on this street. Or that you were still in Florida, for that matter. Last I heard, you were on tap to take command of Joint Task Force Six."

"The Navy made an end run. They're going to fill that slot with one of their own." Regret flickered in his blue eyes, so vivid against his tanned skin. "We haven't exactly kept in touch since the divorce, have we?"

"No, we haven't."

"You said that's how you wanted it."

"I did." She dragged in a long breath. "I still do. I'll break my lease and find another place tomorrow."

In another town. Maybe a different state. No way Andi was going to live next to her ex-husband while she tried to figure out what to do with the rest of her life.

"I know the folks who own that house," Dave said. "They told me they were requiring a hefty security deposit and two months' advance rent. You'll forfeit a big chunk of change if you break the lease."

"Probably."

She'd also have to break the news that she was resettling to her best friend.

Sue Ellen Carson was the one who'd talked Andi into moving to Florida. Like Andi, Sue Ellen was divorced. Twice, in fact. In no hurry to take the plunge again, she'd lured Andi south by dangling promises of long walks on the beach and late nights curled up in front of the TV.

"You don't have to move on my account," Dave said, frowning. "I'm gone a whole lot more than I'm home. As you know."

"Yes, I do."

He scraped a hand across his bristles and tried to find a solution to the dilemma. "Look, my team and I leave next week for a joint exercise. I don't know how long we'll be deployed, but I'm guessing three weeks to a month."

"Just like old times," Andi quipped, hiding a sudden sharp ache behind a wry smile.

"That will give you time to look around, maybe find a way to wiggle out of the lease," Dave argued.

She was too tired after her long drive and too disconcerted by his unexpected reappearance in her life to debate the matter further.

"I'll sleep on it."

She thought about offering him her hand but decided a handshake would be silly after the kiss he'd just laid on her. She settled for another smile.

"It's good to see you again."

"You, too."

"Night, Dave."

She turned to leave, but he stopped her with a, "Hey, Armstrong!"

"Yes?"

Once again the light from the hall silhouetted his muscled frame. Fiercely, Andi quashed the memory of all the times she'd slicked her palms over those hard, sleek contours.

"If you didn't know I lived next door, why did you ring the doorbell?"

"I thought this was a crack house."

"*What?*"

Her sweeping gesture encompassed the weedy front

yard and the shuttered windows. "If you're going to be gone for months at a time, at least hire a yardman to cut the grass. This looks like some of the places I used to drag Carol out of."

Dave was one of the few people she'd told about those awful years, when she'd refused to abandon her only sister to pushers and pimps. He'd admired her stubborn tenacity then. He didn't appear to admire it now.

"Hell, woman! You marched over here after midnight, alone, to confront a possible drug dealer?"

"I wasn't looking for a confrontation. Just some hard evidence before I sicced the cops on you."

When he let loose his favorite expletive, Andi bit her lip. She hadn't heard that particularly scatological epithet in the four years since their divorce. It was unique to Air Force Special Operations.

So was Dave, for that matter. He lived, breathed and slept Special Ops. Andi had known how deep his dedication went when she'd married him. Unfortunately knowing hadn't made the separations shorter or the empty nights any easier to get through.

Shoving aside the painful memories, she popped him a two-fingered salute. "See you around, Armstrong. Maybe."

THAT MAYBE RICOCHETED inside Dave's head like a bullet fired at close range from a M429 SAW. His jaw locking, he watched his ex-wife cross the drive between his house and the one next door. He'd watched Andi walk away from him once before, four years ago. That experience had damn near ripped him apart. This time was worse.

His jaw torquing tighter with her every step, he waited until she was safely inside her house before entering his own. The door slammed hard enough to make the two men in the den shoot questioning looks his way.

Dave didn't enlighten them. This was between Andi and him. And Sue Ellen Carson.

"Hang loose," he instructed the two officers. "I need to make a quick call."

The kitchen door swished shut behind him. Dragging out his cell phone, he punched a speed-dial number. Seconds ticked by, one after another.

"Come on," Dave snarled. "Pick up the damn phone."

Sue Ellen finally answered, her voice thick and chalky. "Whoizzthis?"

"Dave Armstrong. Andi's here."

"Huh?"

"Andi's here."

"She… She can't be. She's, um, on the road. Some-where."

"No, she's not."

They'd been friends once. Dave and Andi, Sue Ellen and her first husband. Unfortunately divorce had a way of separating friends and relatives into opposing camps. Sue Ellen still blamed Dave for the bust-up of his marriage and pretty much cut him off at the knees whenever she saw him. Concern for Andi had turned them into reluctant allies.

"Okay," she muttered. "I'm awake. Sort of. Did you say Andi's here?"

"I did."

"I don't understand. She called from just outside Atlanta and said she was going to stop for the night."

"Obviously she changed her mind."

"But I've got the keys to the house. How did she get in?"

"Beats me."

Knowing his fiercely independent ex, she probably convinced the Realtor to leave a set under the mat rather than roust out her friend late at night.

"Maybe that's not Andi next door. Maybe it's the cleaning crew the Realtor said he'd send in, working late."

"It's Andi, S.E. She marched over and rang my doorbell a few minutes ago."

"Good God!" Panic laced Sue Ellen's soft peaches-and-cream Georgia twang. "She wasn't supposed to find out you live next door until I laid the groundwork."

"That was the plan," Dave agreed. "We need to devise a new one."

"How, er, bad was it?"

Actually, those first few moments were pretty damn good. Dave had forgotten the heat Andrea Joyce Armstrong could spark in his belly with a single kiss.

"Let's just say she wasn't real happy."

Sue Ellen digested that in silence for a few seconds. Dave could almost see her small heart-shaped face screwed up in concentration.

"She said she's going to pack up and leave in the morning. I did my best, S.E., but you're the one who'll have to talk her out of it."

"I will."

"It won't be easy."

"We knew going in this wouldn't be easy. Andi is…well, Andi."

"Yeah," Dave muttered, his gut twisting. "She is."

He snapped the cell phone shut a few moments later, his insides still kinked. They had pretty much stayed that way since Sue Ellen had left an urgent message with his executive officer saying she had to speak with Colonel Armstrong as soon as possible.

Dave had been in the swamp at the time. He spent a lot of time in the swamp. As commander of the 720th Special Tactics Group at Hurlburt Field, home of the Air Force's Special Operations Command, he was responsible for training, equipping and fielding four hundred highly specialized warriors.

In the Army, it was the Rangers. In the Navy, it was the SEALS. In the Air Force, Special Ops went in first. Dave's small, elite cadre of officers and enlisted personnel was trained to infiltrate hostile areas, conduct assault-zone assessment, establish air-traffic control, set up command-and-control communications, remove obstacles or unexploded ordnance and pave the way for air or ground assault forces. Each man carried more than a hundred pounds of equipment and weapons.

Dave's job was to ensure his Special Tactics teams knew theirs. He couldn't do that sitting behind a desk. Like every one of his men, he was high-altitude/low-opening-jump-qualified, scuba-trained, satellite-communications-savvy and a demolitions expert.

He'd put that training to good use during his twenty-three years in Special Ops, participating in more insertions and assaults than he could count. In the process, he'd racked up a chest full of medals and learned to control the bowel-loosening fear that came with each mission. Any man who went in on a mission and didn't admit to fear was either a liar or a fool.

But Dave couldn't remember feeling anything close to the icy terror he'd experienced when he'd returned Sue Ellen's call and learned Andi had been infected with the vicious, drug-resistant *acinetobacter baumannii* bacterium that attacked so many of the troops wounded in Iraq.

Bright, breezy Andi, with her endless energy and enthusiasm for life. She wasn't beautiful. Not by conventional standards. But her sparkling green eyes and ready smile lit up any room she walked into. That same smile had hit Dave like a Sidewinder missile the very first time she'd aimed it his way in the bar at the Kirtland Officers' Club.

Her quick mind and utter dedication to her job had seduced him almost as quickly as her long legs and trim, taut curves. Less than a week after their first meeting, Dave had set out with single-minded deliberation to win her.

Then, four years ago, he'd lost her.

Now Andi had lost the career she'd buried herself in before, during and after their bust-up. She hadn't wanted him to know about the medical eval board. She hadn't wanted anyone to know. Sue Ellen had found out only after a distraught Carol had called her.

So here Andi was, one of the Air Force's youngest and most promising colonels, put out to pasture.

Thank God Sue Ellen had convinced her to come south while she battled that damn bug and adjusted to civilian life. While she did, Dave would team up with S.E. to keep a close eye on her.

Whether Andi wanted him to or not.

CHAPTER 2

Andi woke her first morning in Florida to dazzling sunshine, the bang of a screen door hitting the hinges and a shout from downstairs.

"Andrea Joyce! It's me, girl. Sue Ellen."

Force of habit had Andi rolling over to squint at the digital alarm beside her bed. Only after blinking bleary-eyed at the empty nightstand did she remember this wasn't her bed and she hadn't gotten around to unpacking her travel clock last night. The long drive and unexpected face-to-face with Dave had disconcerted her so much she'd left her suitcases right where she'd deposited them. All she'd done was dig through the box of linens she'd carried in from the car for a set of sheets and a towel.

"Haul your *behind* down to the kitchen!" Sue Ellen's Georgia drawl gave the command its own cadence. "I brought coffee and Krispy Kremes."

The last two magic words produced an instant reaction from Andi. "I'm on my way!"

Slithering out of the sinfully soft six-hundred-thread Egyptian cotton sheets she'd purchased in a moment of sheer indulgence, she made a quick detour to the master bath.

She hadn't had time to give it more than a cursory inspection last night. Then, she'd approved of its spaciousness and layout. In the bright light of day, she got her first good look at its elegance.

The sunlight streaming through the skylight set above the sinks showed a pastel-pink-and-pale-turquoise color scheme accented with the same seaside motif used throughout the rest of the house. The scalloped sink bowls looked like gleaming clamshells. Tall, feathery sea grasses sprouted from a wicker basket. Best of all, the window above the hot tub offered a glimpse of rolling sand dunes and the green waters of the Gulf of Mexico.

Drawn by the lure of coffee and doughnuts, Andi didn't bother to do more than splash cold water on her face and attack her fuzzy teeth. Finger-combing her shoulder-length brown bob, she made for the stairs. The hardwood treads felt cool and smooth under her bare soles. By contrast, Sue Ellen's greeting was warm and joyous.

The petite blonde flung herself across the spacious kitchen to envelope Andi in a fierce hug and a cloud of Chanel No. 5. "I'm so glad you're finally here."

Andi returned her hug with unrestrained affection. "Me, too."

She and S.E. had been close pals for more than fifteen years—a rarity in the military, where constant moves made for a multitude of acquaintances but few enduring friendships. They'd not only kept in touch, they'd shared each other's highs and lows.

Sue Ellen had been an Air Force spouse and a lowly GS-3 when she and Andi had first met at Randolph AFB, outside San Antonio. Despite her college degree, S.E. had had to restart at the bottom of the civil service ladder and take whatever job she could find after each of her husband's transfers. Since dumping Charlie, she'd gone to work for the Department of Labor, shot up the ranks to the exalted grade of GS-12 and now headed DOL's regional office in Pensacola, some twenty miles east of Gulf Springs. Along the way, she'd met, married and dumped husband number two.

"Here." Retrieving a foam cup from the counter, she shoved it into Andi's eager hand. "Strong and black, the way you like it. And this," she said, digging a French cruller out of the red-and-green checkered box, "is gooey and sweet, just the way I like it."

Sue Ellen downed half the confection with gusto before leveling an accusing look at her friend. "Why didn't you call me last night and let me know you'd decided to drive on in?"

"Because I didn't decide until late."

"How'd you get into the house?"

"I had the Realtor FedEx me a set of keys before I left D.C."

"You didn't tell me 'bout that, either. I went by his office yesterday and picked up a set. I was going to have this place all aired out and ready for you."

"It's ready enough."

More than ready, Andi thought, glancing around the cheerful kitchen. Sunlight danced through oyster-white plantation shutters. The antiseptic scent of pine cleaner still lingered on the counters. There wasn't a trace of the damp or mold so prevalent in homes along the humid Gulf coast, not to mention the inevitable mosquitoes and palmetto bugs. The cleaning crew the Realtor had sent in had done their job well.

Sliding onto one of the counter stools, Andi helped herself to a raspberry-filled doughnut and bit in. The sugar jolted straight to her system. "Did you know Dave's assignment to CENTAF was canceled?"

S.E. downed the rest of her cruller in a quick, guilty gulp. "I, uh, heard something about it."

"And you didn't tell me because…?"

"I didn't think it would matter one way or another. You never mention the man or have anything to do with him."

Andi let that pass, mostly because it was true, and zeroed in on the greater crime.

"Answer me this. When I called to tell you the Realtor had found this rental for me, did you know Dave lived right next door?"

"No! I swear!"

"Sue Ellen…"

"Honest to God, Andi. I knew he was in the area, but I've seen him maybe twice in the past two years—and then only in passing. I didn't have a clue where he lived until I drove over here to take a look at this place and saw the weedy, overgrown yard next door. I was worried you might get stuck with bad neighbors, so I called the Realtor. He said the house belonged to a Special Ops type who was gone a lot and, um, sort of mentioned Dave's name."

"Dammit, Sue Ellen!" Anger and hurt ripped through Andi. "We're supposed to be best friends. How could you let me move in here knowing he lived next door?"

"I wouldn't have, except Dave understands how these medical evaluation boards work and…"

"You talked to him about the eval board?"

"I figured he'd give me the straight scoop about how the process worked. Then I told him you were thinking of moving down here and, well…"

S.E. hunched her shoulders, looking guilty and miserable and worried all at the same time.

"We didn't know how serious this bug is. We figured the more friends you had around you right now, the better."

"Dave and I are not friends. We're—we're…"

"Yes?"

"Ex-lovers. Former spouses. Fellow officers." Andi searched for the right tag. After the kiss Dave had laid on her last night, none seemed to fit. "Hell, I don't know what we are anymore."

"For all his faults, the man cares about you, girlfriend. He always has."

To her utter disgust, Andi felt the hot sting of tears. Dave *cared* about her. He'd once loved her with such greedy, all-consuming passion he couldn't get enough of her, morning, noon or night.

"This isn't going to work, Sue Ellen. I can't live next to him."

"Why not?"

"I came to Florida to start a new life, not wallow around in my old one."

"I'm part of your old one." Hurt colored her friend's pansy-purple eyes. "Are you saying you don't want me to be part of your new life?"

"Of course not. I wouldn't be here if I felt that way."

"Then what's the problem? You're in control of the situation. You let Dave into this new life only as much as you want to."

"The problem is that things could get awkward." Just in time, Andi caught a glob of raspberry filling with a finger and transferred both to her mouth. "What if he's seeing someone? How does he explain the ex-wife next door?"

"He's not. And if he was, he'd handle the situation the same way you will when *you* start seeing someone. By the way, what happened with that White House staffer? You left me hanging after your second date."

"I sort of left him hanging, too."

"Too bad. He sounded really hot."

"He was, but he had as much or more on his plate as I did on mine."

"Speaking of which…"

S.E. reached across the counter and tipped Andi's chin to view the tiny scar.

"Okay, so what's the deal? When do you go in for your next blood test?"

"Next week. I have to call and make an appointment."

Andi was supposed to have her blood checked every other week and consult with a cardiologist every other month. So far the damage to her heart muscle had been minimal. She wanted to keep it that way.

"That gives us the rest of this week to get you settled and play," Sue Ellen announced.

"Us? You've still got a job, remember?"

"I took the rest of the week off."

"I thought you had that big conference at DOL head-quarters to prepare for?"

She dismissed the conference she'd worried and fussed over the phone about with a wave of one manicured hand. "That's what staff are for. Okay, here's my suggestion. Let's walk down to the beach. If that doesn't convince you to stay, nothing will."

"I saw a glimpse of it from the bathroom window," Andi admitted.

"I'm telling you, girl, you'll be in heaven on that beach. Since I intend to spend most of my free time here with you, I will, too. I bought new floaties, stocked up on Diet Coke and have a whole stack of romances ready and waitin'. It'll be just like old times."

Andi remembered saying the same thing to Dave last night. Swallowing, she forced a grin. "Not quite. At least this time we won't be floating in six inches of water."

"Oh, God! You still remember that kiddie pool?"

"How could I forget?"

S.E. had bought the plastic child's pool to defeat the brutal Texas heat one long ago summer. It had fit her petite frame with room to spare. At five-eight, Andi had draped over either side.

They'd spent hours in that pool with their books and drinks. Andi could still remember the sizzling afternoon Sue Ellen had convinced her to abandon gory thrillers and try one of her romance novels. Andi had been hooked ever since.

She had to admit the prospect of doing nothing but lying on the beach and reading held a distinct appeal. For a few weeks or months, anyway. Until she knew what direction her life would take.

First, though, she had to decide whether she'd stay here in Gulf Springs.

A TREK DOWN TO THE shore decided the issue.

The housing development edged a public beach. Narrow paths cut through dunes topped by feathery sea oats. Beyond the dunes, rolling green waves lapped at sand so white and dazzling the women had to shield their eyes against the glare.

"Oh, God!" Sue Ellen was in near ecstasy. "If you move out of your house, I'm going to move in."

"You can't afford it. Not until that gigolo you divorced last year finds a job and you can stop paying alimony."

"Which doesn't look like it's going to happen anytime soon." S.E.'s expressive face screwed into a grimace. "Henrik looked and dressed and behaved so elegantly. Why didn't I see past all that to the scuzzball underneath?"

"Because he made his living by looking and dressing and behaving elegantly. And by marrying well. You were—what?—his third or fourth wife?"

"Fourth," S.E. confirmed with a sigh. "Sure wish I'd hired a private investigator to check him out *before* he drained my bank account. I won't make that mistake again. What about you?" she asked. "Can you afford that rental house on half pay?"

"It's a stretch," Andi admitted.

More than a stretch. It was an out-and-out extravagance. Luckily her D.C. condo had sold for considerably more than she'd anticipated. She could dip into the profits from the sale until she found another source of income to augment her greatly reduced retired pay. Considering how her world had turned so suddenly and so completely upside down, Andi figured she deserved a little extravagance.

The house might be a stretch, but the beach became an instant necessity. Kicking off her flip-flops, she plowed through the sand to the shore. Waves curled in lace-capped green waves. The surf tickled her toes.

She needed this, Andi realized as the ocean breeze played with the ends of her hair. These restless waves. The long stretch of deserted beach. The vast emptiness.

Her life had been so full up to now. And so regimented. For the first time in twenty-one years she wouldn't have to measure her days by the military's twenty-four-hour clock or spit-shine her boots or keep her hair off her collar. Nor would she carry the heavy burden of command, with its addictive power and 24-7 pressure.

She hadn't really had time to think about jettisoning the stress she'd carted around for so long. But now, staring at those mesmerizing waves, she could almost feel the weight of it roll off her back.

With her new weightlessness came a dawning realization. She could get up when she wanted to. Read all night if she chose to. Sit here in this soft, sugary sand and just watch the sea.

"I'm staying," she told Sue Ellen. "For now."

"Yippeee!" Kicking up a shower of sand and surf, her friend did a happy dance. "Let's get you settled in."

UNPACKING THE SUITCASES and boxes Andi had brought with her in the Tahoe took only a few hours. The moving van hauling her furniture and household goods was scheduled to arrive later that afternoon. Andi used the time in between to conduct a thorough inventory of the house and decide which of her own pieces she'd use and which would go into storage.

By seven that evening the two women had almost everything in place. Andi hunkered down on the living room floor to sort through her stack of CDs, while Sue Ellen flopped onto the sofa and shot her an accusing look.

"I thought the docs warned you that you'd run out of steam more easily than you did before that bug crawled into your heart."

"That's what they said."

"So when do you start?" Sue Ellen huffed.

Andi wasn't about to admit she'd already started. Ignoring the pulsing ache just under her breastbone, she arranged the CDs next to the handy-dandy little box that was a combination of stereo, AM/FM radio, CD player and iPod dock.

"There. We're done."

She sat back on her heels and surveyed the high-ceilinged room. With her books lining the white-painted built-in bookshelves and her collection of Swarovski crystal critters displayed in a glass-fronted curio cabinet, the house already felt like home.

A yawning Sue Ellen stretched both arms above her head. Her tank top separated from her shorts, exposing the diamond nestled in her belly button. Andi blinked at the glittering stud.

"When did you get that?"

"A couple weeks ago. I figured I might as well do something with my engagement ring from number two. Especially since I paid for it." Contorting into a U, Sue Ellen contemplated her navel. "Looks good, doesn't it?"

"It's, uh, eye-catching."

"You should get a belly ring or stud. Something in emeralds to match your eyes."

"Not allowed."

The automatic reply slipped out before Andi remembered she didn't have to conform to the Air Force's uniform regulations anymore. She could have any part of her pierced or tattooed she wanted. Not that she wanted either. Still, it came as a small shock to think that her body—like her life—was now her own.

"What do you want to do for supper?" Sue Ellen asked with another joint-cracking stretch. "I hear a great new seafood place just opened in Navarre Beach."

"I'm all gritty and sweaty. How about we just order in a pizza?"

"That works for me. Mushrooms, onions and green peppers on my half. You make the call while I fetch us something cold to drink."

She returned a few moments later with two champagne flutes.

"I brought a bottle of '03 Piper-Heidsieck with me. Thought we should celebrate your arrival in style."

After shedding husband number two, Sue Ellen had joined a wine club in an attempt to expand her interests and put her old life behind her. In the process, she'd developed a passion for fine vintages.

Andi, on the other hand, couldn't tell the difference between a $6.99 supermarket brand and a hundred-dollar label. She suspected this Piper-whatever would go down like the nectar of the gods. Unfortunately she couldn't sample it.

"I'd better stick to Diet Coke. I'm not supposed to drink alcohol while I'm taking these antibiotics."

"Oh, shit! I'm sorry. I didn't think about that."

"Hey, it's no big deal. Just the opposite, in fact. I've lost five pounds since I gave up beer and margaritas."

Sue Ellen kept her thoughts to herself as she went back to the kitchen to trade champagne for diet cola, but she couldn't help worrying whether her friend's weight loss was due to more than just abstinence from alcohol.

Andi *seemed* healthy enough. Her eyes held the same sparkle they always had. Her sun-streaked brown hair showed a glossy sheen. Tall and trim, she carried herself with the same athletic grace and unconscious air of authority she always had, in or out of uniform. Yet the medical evaluation board had deemed her condition serious enough to mandate retirement from active military service.

Since learning about Andi's condition, Sue Ellen had spent countless hours on Google looking up articles about subacute viral endocarditis, the condition Andi had developed as a result of that damn bug. She'd struggled through descriptions of the various forms of the disease and associated treatments, which might ultimately require replacement of damaged heart valves.

Most patients had to be hospitalized for long periods and treated with massive doses of antibiotics administered intravenously. In rare instances, highly motivated patients with a previously stable heart and a viral-type infection could be treated at home.

Andi was nothing if not highly motivated.

Sue Ellen knew Dave had done his own extensive research and consulted the cardiologist at the base who'd been faxed Andi's medical records. The doc couldn't violate patient-physician confidentiality, of course, but she had helped Dave understand the parameters of the disease. Dave, in turn, had explained it to Sue Ellen. Strange how concern for Andi had bridged the gap spawned by the divorce.

Thank God Andi had agreed to come to Florida instead of moving to Ohio to be close to her older sister. Carol was smart and savvy but had troubles of her own. She was also no good in a crisis, as she'd be the first to admit.

The roar of a powerful engine pulled Sue Ellen from her thoughts.

"What the heck…?"

The deafening thunder drew both women to the living room windows, where they spotted a riding mower chugging across the lawn next door. Dave sat in the driver's seat, his back bare to the still-hot evening sun. New-mown grass dusted the gleaming skin.

"'Bout time he cut those weeds," Andi commented. "I must have shamed him into it."

Sue Ellen hooked a brow. "That's what you guys discussed when you went over there last night? Weeds?"

She knew she'd made a mistake when Andi turned to her with a frown creasing her brow.

"Who said I went over there?"

"You must have mentioned it."

"No, I didn't."

"You sure? I distinctly remember us talking about him this morning, at the kitchen counter."

"About him, yes, but I never said I went to his place— last night or any other time."

Her angry glance swept to the man on the mower and back again.

"Dammit, Sue Ellen. What's going on here? Have you and my ex-husband formed some sort of unholy alliance?"

Caught, she could only admit the truth. "Not an alliance, exactly. More like a loose confederation."

"But you don't even *like* him."

"Hey, he damn near broke your heart. That makes him scum in my book."

Sue Ellen had never bought Andi's stubborn contention that the divorce was by mutual agreement. She'd been through two herself. The hurt was inescapable.

"The point is, Dave is as worried about you as I am. That puts us on the same side."

Andi's mouth folded into a thin line. "I didn't come down here to be worried about or fussed over."

"I know, I know. We won't fuss. I promise. And we won't intrude. We just feel better knowing one of us is only a shout away."

Some of the stiffness went out of her friend's back. Sue Ellen swallowed a sigh of relief and played her trump card.

"Dave won't impose, Andi. And he won't be watching you through the windows. He told me he's got some sort of deployment coming up."

"He told me the same thing."

"There you are, then. You probably won't see much of him until he goes, but you'll know he's nearby…if you need him," she tacked on hastily.

CHAPTER 3

Sue Ellen's blithe prediction that Andi wouldn't see much of her ex got shot all to hell the very next morning. She not only saw him, she saw a whole lot more of him than she wanted or needed to.

She woke early, still on a military schedule, and took her coffee down to the beach. Although the sun was just a hazy red ball hanging low in the sky, the temperature was already pushing seventy. A warm breeze rustled through the tall sea oats. The feathery stalks brushed Andi's thighs under the ragged hem of her cutoffs when she took the path through the dunes.

Once past the dunes, she kicked off her flip-flops. Sand curled through her toes as she carried her shoes and coffee mug to the eddying surf. Except for the fisherman trolling far down the beach, she might have been alone in the universe. Turning her back on the angler, she left a trail of footsteps that filled up and disappeared with each new wave.

Just like life, she thought wryly. You make a niche for

yourself. Carve out your own special pattern. Then a wave washes in and gradually obliterates it. Or not so gradually. Her wave had slammed down without warning, carrying all the force of a tsunami.

Since then, the realization that she'd have to carve a new pattern had rolled around inside her belly like a lead ball. For some reason, though, the queasy feeling seemed to have dissipated.

Maybe because she'd severed the cord and put the Pentagon behind her. Or because she'd left D.C., with its frantic traffic and constant obsession with itself. Or just because she was strolling through the surf on a warm, hazy morning with nothing more pressing to do than hook up her computer and notify folks of her new address.

"I can handle that," she informed the seagull who swooped in for a landing a few yards away.

A second gull landed beside the first and fluffed its feathers. Both birds trailed after Andi, their heads cocked in expectation.

"Sorry, guys. All I have with me is coffee. I'll bring some goodies tomorrow."

Looking thoroughly disgusted, the gulls flapped off. A busy little sandpiper took their place. Darting in and out of the water, the tiny, bright-eyed creature wove a network of spidery tracks.

Smiling at its antics, Andi found a spot out of the reach of the eddy and plopped down. Her bare feet burrowed into the sand. Her elbows rested on her knees.

She could handle this, too, she thought. Early-morning walks along the beach. Glorious sunrises. Not another human in sight except the fisherman and the jogger now splashing through the surf a mile or more away.

Turning her face to the sea, she sipped her coffee. She was lost in contemplation of the sun burning through the haze and burnishing the sea into an endless vista of emerald laced with sparkling diamonds when the jogger entered her field of vision. From the corner of one eye she saw his long, easy stride slow, then check.

"Andi?"

Oh, no! She wasn't ready for another meeting with her ex-husband. She still hadn't sorted through their first one. Swallowing a groan, she put up a hand to shield her eyes and squinted through the shimmering heat already rising from the sand.

The other night Dave had presented her with an up-close-and-personal view of his bare chest. This morning the chest was covered—more or less—by a gray T-shirt with the sleeves ripped out for ventilation. His black Lycra biker shorts left most of the rest of him available for view, however, and emphasized the bulge between his thighs.

Wrenching her gaze upward, Andi managed a cool smile. "Morning, Dave. Changed your routine, I see. You used to run in the evening."

He'd always claimed a long run relieved the stress of the day. It also brought him home drenched with sweat and pumping pure endorphins. As Andi knew all too well, those busy little neurotransmitters induced a sense of euphoria popularly called "runner's high." In the process, they stimulated the release of sexual hormones.

She couldn't count the number of times Dave had seduced, sweet-talked or just plain swept her off her feet for a bout of steamy postrun sex. The sudden graphic memory of one unforgettable session on the kitchen counter set *her* endorphins to sparking and snapping.

"I still run in the evening when I get the chance," Dave said, jerking her thoughts away from scattered appliances and cool, smooth marble. "I'm flying this evening, so I figured I'd better get my run in early."

"Oh. Well. Don't let me keep you."

"No problem. I've logged my miles."

Uninvited, he dropped down beside her. The tang of well-worn running shoes and healthy male sweat competed with that of damp sand and salty air.

"What kind of flight do you have?" she asked, more to take her mind off the muscled calves stretched out beside hers than to make conversation.

"We're looking at a new avionics package for the H-model MC-130. I'm dropping a team of combat controllers to see how compatible the avionics are with our pathfinder satellite system."

"Is this a HALO drop?"

She'd learned to speak Special Ops-ese during their years together. HALO for high altitude, low opening. HAHO for high altitude, high opening. CCT for combat control team. MATC for mobile air traffic control. All the acronyms that defined Dave's life.

"This one's a night free fall."

"Into the gulf?"

"Another puddle of water," was all he would say.

"So they'll have to inflate their rubber duck," Andi murmured, visualizing the team's plunge from a low-flying aircraft into dark, unfamiliar waters and subsequent scramble into an inflatable raft.

"That," Dave agreed, "or sink like stones. We've added another eight pounds of equipment to the hundred-plus they already carry in their rucksacks."

She winced in sympathy. To earn their coveted scarlet berets, his combat controllers went into austere and often dangerous locations carrying everything necessary to establish an airfield and direct aircraft. In addition to chemical gear, parachutes, scuba equipment, radios and weapons, they lugged portable runway lights and a motorcycle they could assemble in minutes for swift travel over rough terrain.

His other special-tactics teams went in similarly burdened with specialized equipment. The PJs—pararescuemen—more than earned their maroon headgear, the combat weathermen their distinctive gray berets.

"I heard the personnel from the 23rd were involved in last month's rescue of a downed RAF pilot in the mountains north of Kandahar," Andi commented.

"Yeah." Dave scrubbed a hand over his face. "That one was a bitch."

While the waves danced in and out, he shared the details of that particularly hairy mission, and the awkwardness between them faded in the familiarity of military operations.

They'd always had this, Andi thought as she listened to the familiar rhythm of his voice. Shared careers. A common knowledge of people and places and weapons systems. Understanding of the sometimes overwhelming burden of responsibility each of them carried.

How had they let those grinding responsibilities build into the wedge that drove them apart? When had their priorities gotten so screwed up that their jobs had become more important than each other?

Okay, there was the small matter of a war being fought on several fronts. Not to mention highly specialized training, ever-increasing rank and a commitment to their troops that went bone deep. The higher she and Dave went in rank, the deeper that commitment ran.

Kids would have forced them to reorder their priorities, Andi thought with a dart of pain.

They'd certainly planned to have children. At first. They'd kept putting it off, waiting for the right time to start a family. Then it was too late. The cracks in their marriage were already showing. Neither she nor Dave wanted to bring children into an uncertain home, particularly with both of them gone so much.

Oh, well. No point rehashing old regrets. Shoving those painful years out of her head, she said little as Dave described the aftermath of the rescue mission.

"When we got him back to base, the Brits had a reception committee waiting. Our guys transferred him to an aerovac flight to the screech of 'Wild Blue Yonder' as interpreted by a former member of the RAF Halton Pipe and Drum Corps."

A smile played at the corners of Andi's mouth as she envisioned the dusty airfield high in the mountains of Afghanistan. The wail of a bagpipe would echo across the runways and be heard for miles. She'd bet more than one turbaned head had whipped around in surprise.

"I saw the RAF Halton Pipe and Drum Corps perform at the Edinburgh military tattoo some years back," she commented. "They gave me goose bumps."

"They gave a few of the locals around Kandahar goose bumps, too."

Hooking her arms around her raised knees, she surveyed the emerald-green sea. "This is sure a long way from that part of the world, isn't it?"

"Yeah, it is."

A long way from the Pentagon and the organization of the Joint Chiefs of Staff, as well. She and Dave might have been on another planet. The air around them didn't buzz with urgency. There were no decision papers to push through, no briefings to prepare for, no harried staffers making Andi's life miserable with yet another change to a time-phased deployment schedule.

"Funny," she murmured, resting her chin on her knees. "I never pictured myself sitting on a beach with nothing more pressing to do for the rest of the day than hook up my computer. I always thought I'd have a clear picture of what I wanted to do after the Air Force and march quickstep into a new life. Now I don't know what direction I'm marching in."

"You'll figure it out, babe."

"You think?"

"I know. This is just a temporary right oblique."

A half angle to the right, executed with military precision? Andi didn't think so. It felt more like a rout step.

She didn't voice her doubts, however. She'd already

come off sounding way too much like a wimp. They sat in silence until Dave checked his watch.

"Guess I'd better clean up and get ready for work. You heading back to the house?"

"I'll stay in the sun for a while."

"Take it easy the first few times out."

"Yes, sir."

"You don't want to burn."

"No, sir."

"Smart-ass."

"If you say so, sir."

Grinning, he got to his feet and dusted off, showering her with fine white sand in the process.

"See you around, Armstrong."

"If you're lucky, Armstrong."

The old retort popped out before she could catch it. Administering a mental head shake, Andi stretched out her legs and wiggled her toes. Dave started for the path that cut through the dunes but halted a few yards away.

"When do you see the cardiologist?"

"Next week."

"Keep me posted," he ordered tersely.

Andi thought about reminding him she didn't have to follow orders any longer, his or anyone else's. She settled for a noncommittal grunt and planted her elbows in the sand. Eyes closed, she tipped her face to the sun.

THAT WAS THE IMAGE Dave took into the shower with him: his wife with her head back and her throat arched.

Ex-wife, he corrected, his belly clenching.

It still hit him like that every time he thought of the divorce. Andi was the one who'd insisted they legalize the separation. Dave would've hung in there, toughed it out until they'd come up with a workable compromise. Problem was, they were never in the same place at the same time long enough to hammer one out. So he'd packed his hurt along with his bruised pride, accepted another overseas assignment and left Andi to find someone new.

She'd had four years to accomplish that.

Four friggin' years.

She almost found him. The news she was engaged had hit Dave like a runaway Abrams tank. He'd sucked it up, told himself that Andi deserved days filled with happiness, hoped she'd found it with this guy. He'd even sent her an e-mail spouting some drivel like that.

He hadn't meant a word of it. Every pound of the keyboard had torqued his jaw tighter and tighter. He would rather have used pliers to tear off his own fingernails one by one than type that damned e-mail. He never heard why the engagement fizzled, and didn't care. All that mattered was Andi was here, back in his life.

"No more e-mails, Andrea Joyce. You're on my turf now."

FOR THE NEXT FEW DAYS Andi made it a point to take her walks later in morning, when she was sure Dave would have already left for work.

She'd enjoyed those quiet moments with him more than she should have. For that brief interval they'd put the old hurts aside. She didn't want to risk new ones, however. Not with everything else she had to sort through right now.

The first critical sorting came with her doctor's appointment the following Thursday. She'd done her blood work the day before. Now she faced the verdict as delivered by the cardiologist. Her appointment was at fifteen-twenty.

She'd written 3:20 p.m. on her calendar in an effort to force herself to think civilian, but driving across the Navarre Bridge and through the front gates of Hurlburt Field plunged her right back into the military.

Security-force personnel bristling with SAWs and sidearms guarded the front gate. Troops in desert BDUs hurried about their business. Low-flying C-130 gunships buzzed in for landing on the runway that bisected the base.

Once an auxiliary field to sprawling Eglin Air Force Base just twelve miles away, Hurlburt had always been considered a sort of stepchild. The base had come into its own with the emergence of Special Ops as a major arm of force employment. Modern buildings had replaced the old clapboard structures. New facilities had sprung up everywhere. HQ, USAF Special Operations Command occupied a gleaming steel-and-glass high-rise.

The runway was now crowded with Pavehawk and Pavelow helicopters and every configuration of the workhorse of the Air Force—the fixed-wing four-engine C-130 Hercules. As Andi circled the end of the runway and headed for the east side of the base, another heavily armed gunship lifted off and seemed to skim right over her head.

With a regional hospital so close by at Eglin, Hurlburt was served by a walk-in clinic staffed with medical personnel trained to go into the field with the combat-hardened troops they served. Active-duty military received first priority. Their families, although vital, had to come second. Retirees ranked third on the list and often received care on a space-available basis only.

Still struggling to get used to her new status, Andi had prepared herself for a long wait. The clinic's prompt efficiency was a pleasant surprise. A corpsman in sharp-creased BDUs called her for her appointment right on time.

"We haven't had a cardiologist on staff for almost a year," he told Andi as he escorted her down a tiled hall smelling of antiseptic and pine cleaner. "We're lucky Dr. Ramirez just rotated back from Korea. If you'll have a seat on the exam table, Colonel, I'll take your vitals."

After recording the results on a chart, he left her to swing her legs and wait for the doc. Ramirez entered a few moments later, carrying a thick file. Her subdued rank insignia identified her as a lieutenant colonel. The wreathed star on her flight surgeon's wings indicated she'd racked up a good number of years' experience in the highly specialized field of aviation medicine.

"Hello, Colonel Armstrong. I'm Dr. Ramirez. I know your husband. Excuse me—former husband."

Andi smiled and shrugged aside the small awkwardness. Special Ops was a relatively small community. She'd often bumped into friends or associates of Dave's. Some knew they were divorced, some didn't.

"How have you been feeling?"

"Pretty darn good, actually."

"No dizziness? Shortness of breath? Pain in your chest cavity?"

"No. Well, once. I felt a small ache after I finished unpacking my household goods."

"Mmm." All business now, Ramirez placed the file on the exam room's counter. "Your physician at the Pentagon faxed me your history. I've reviewed your EKGs, nuclear treadmill tests, echocardiograms and MRIs. I've also studied the results of your latest blood test. Let me listen to your heart, then we'll talk."

The stethoscope was cool against Andi's skin, the flight

surgeon thorough. She listened intently for long moments before hooking the instrument around her neck again.

"Your heartbeat sounds good. Very strong and steady."

Andi sagged with relief. The docs had warned her the infection she'd picked up could cause an irregular heartbeat. Arrhythmia often caused the heart to pump so fast or so erratically that the chambers didn't have time to fill. That, in turn, meant insufficient blood pumped to the brain and other organs.

Arrhythmia could be lethal, especially among athletes and others who regularly stressed their bodies to the max. Just last year Maggie Dixon, the twenty-eight-year-old coach of the Army women's basketball team, had collapsed and died during a game.

The military had long recognized the impact of strenuous physical training and combat-related stress on the heart, but advances in electronic record keeping were expanding that knowledge by exponential degrees. Along with almost three hundred thousand other military troops, Andi had participated in the groundbreaking and still ongoing Postdeployment Medical Assessment. She and other military personnel who'd served overseas had been screened for everything from syphilis to post-traumatic stress disorder.

It was during this postdeployment screening that Andi learned she'd brought an unwanted, unwelcome bug home with her. She was only one of hundreds of American troops now having to deal with the sand-borne bacterium.

"Your strong, steady heartbeat is the good news," Dr. Ramirez warned, her dark eyes grave. "The not-so-good news is that your blood work still shows traces of *acineto-bacter baumannii*."

"That little sucker is proving to be one tough bastard."

"Yes, it is. I've consulted with specialists at Bethesda. I want to try you on a different mix of antibiotics. I'll also schedule you for another MRI. In the meantime, try not to overstress."

"What's to stress, Doc? I'm retired."

"I suspect you didn't make colonel by taking life easy," the flight surgeon said dryly. "You may have to work at it."

"Trust me, I am. I don't plan anything more strenuous than walks on the beach and catching up on my reading."

That was her intent, anyway.

By the end of her third week in Florida, Andi had discovered that she was constitutionally incapable of a life of ease.

CHAPTER 4

"I'm going nutso, Sue Ellen."

Grumbling, Andi propped her bottle of iced green tea on her middle and shifted in her lounger. This was the third weekend she and S.E. had lugged chairs, umbrella and a cooler down to the beach. The first had been wonderful, all dazzling sunshine and sparkling waves. The second had drifted by at the same lazy pace. By the third, the novelty was fast wearing off.

"I've read every new release in the library and practically cleaned out that dingy little bookstore in Navarre. I've got to find something to do with my time."

Sighing, Sue Ellen pushed up the brim of her floppy hat. The diamond in her belly button shot off a zillion colorful sparks as she angled toward her friend. She and Andi had had this discussion several times. Each time, the options narrowed a little more.

"We've talked about this. Volunteer work at the hospital is out. You can't risk working around patients and picking up another form of infection."

"Ditto volunteering just about everywhere else. You and I and the docs know I'm not contagious, but I wouldn't blame employers for getting a tad nervous when I tell them I'm on antibiotics."

"Nothing says you *have* to tell them. As you point out, you're not infectious."

"Still, there are things like medical insurance and liability to consider. I wouldn't want someone working for me who neglected to mention a small thing like 'the curse.'"

That's what they'd taken to calling the persistent little bug. The curse. Andi had other names for it, but none she could repeat in public.

"What about your idea for an Internet-based bookstore?" Sue Ellen asked.

S.E. knew she wouldn't be able to rein her friend in much longer. She'd used up almost all her wheedling and cajoling skills to sit on the woman for this long. Of all the schemes Andi had come up with as an outlet for her restless energy, Sue Ellen figured running an Internet-based business from a beach home *might* be the least stressful.

"Have you given that any more thought?"

"Matter of fact, I've done more than just think about it."

Sue Ellen slid her sunglasses to the tip of her nose. "Is that so?"

"I've been researching what it would take to establish

an account with several major book distributors. I've also analyzed the profitability of selling via the Internet, with its associated shipping costs, versus in-store sales."

"In-store? You mean like a bookshop?"

"Right. I could reach a much larger customer base through the Internet, but the profit margin is greater with in-store sales. Plus, a shop would get me out of the house."

Sue Ellen didn't like the sound of this. She suspected Dave Armstrong would like it even less. Before he'd departed for his deployment, the colonel had issued strict orders to his reluctant coconspirator: S.E. was to keep Andi relaxed and stress free until his return. Frowning, she peered at her friend over the rims of her sunglasses.

"You're not thinking of opening an actual store, are you?"

"Well…"

"You don't know how long you'll remain on the retired list, Andi. Why would you want to invest time, energy and money in a business you might have to abandon?"

"*Because* I don't know how long I'll remain on the list. It could be a year. It could be forever. I can't just sit here and twiddle my thumbs."

"But a shop," Sue Ellen protested. "You'd have to deal with employees and set hours and cranky customers. You don't need that kind of hassle."

"It doesn't have to be a hassle."

Dislodging the bottle of green tea, Andi wiggled upright in her beach chair. The ideas that had been swirling around in her head for the past week spilled out, taking shape and color as she spoke.

"I'd take a short-term lease and apply for a small-business loan instead of investing my own savings. It would be a small store selling the latest bestsellers, with an associated online order business. Customers could walk in and browse the shelves. If they didn't find what they wanted, they could sit down at a computer terminal, place an order right then and there and have the books shipped directly to their home."

"Combining the best of both worlds," Sue Ellen murmured. "The pleasure of leafing through bookshelves and the instant gratification of ordering exactly what you want online."

"Precisely! I've checked into bar-code-scanning equipment and software. With minor modifications, I could use the same software for ordering and controlling inventory."

"Good grief! You really have been thinking about this."

"I have. And the more I think, the more excited I get."

"I just can't see you stuck behind a counter all day, every day."

"It wouldn't be every day. I'd hire someone to work it for me. As a matter of fact, I've already got an employee lined up."

"Who?"

"The woman who works in that bookstore in Navarre. She wants out of there in the worst way."

"But—but…you'd have to obtain business permits and a sales tax permit and liability insurance and God knows what else."

"Figuring all that out will be half the fun."

"You say that now. You might feel differently six months from now."

"I might. Then again, I might be having the time of my life."

Andi could see from the expression on Sue Ellen's face that her friend was fast running out of arguments. In desperation, S.E. pulled out one more.

"What about the stress?"

"Come on, S.E. What stress? Compared to the job I just left at the Pentagon, the book business will be a piece of cake."

"You think?"

"I know." Lifting her hand, Andi ticked off her rationale finger by finger. "First, my decisions won't impact thousands of troops worldwide. Only me and maybe a part-time helper. Second, I'll be my own boss for the first time in my life. I can set my own hours, work as little or as long as I want. Third, I can diddly-bop into work wearing jeans or shorts or whatever instead of Class A's or BDUs. Best of all," she concluded with a grin, "I'll be up to my ears in books. Talk about a chocoholic turned loose in a candy store."

Sue Ellen chewed on her lower lip. "Sounds like you've made up your mind."

"Pretty much."

"Have you talked to Dave about this?"

That threw Andi a curveball. Blinking, she tossed it right back. "Why would I?"

"I just thought since the two of you are on speaking terms again, you might, you know…discuss things."

"I've seen Dave exactly three times since I arrived in Florida. That first night, the next morning here on the beach and when he was loading his gear into the trunk of his car to leave for a joint exercise."

Andi refused to admit she missed him. Although they'd crossed paths only a few times, knowing he lived right next door gave her a crazy sense of security.

Nor could she admit she'd lain awake a few nights thinking about the hard, hot press of his mouth on hers. Sue Ellen would pounce on that like a rat on a chunk of cheddar.

"This is my decision. When and if I see any reason to tell Dave, I will."

Squirming, her friend slid her glasses back up and took refuge behind them. Andi plucked them off her nose.

"Don't make me hurt you, girl. Promise you'll keep this between us."

"Okay, okay. Just be prepared for some heavy-duty explaining when Dave finds out. He's not going to be happy."

"So he's not happy." Exasperated, Andi pushed out of her beach chair. "Last I heard, Dave Armstrong and I were divorced."

"In your mind, maybe," Sue Ellen muttered under her breath as she rose and gathered her things.

ANDI TRIED TO PACE herself over the next few weeks. She honestly tried.

She took her time devising a strategic plan with an associated checklist of items to be accomplished. When she finished, the plan filled a three-ring binder and included detailed spreadsheets, timelines and color-coded tabs for each phase of activity.

Phase one involved investigating start-up costs for the type of business she had in mind. Andi soon had a working estimate that included shop rental, utilities and purchase of her initial inventory. Her next step was to contact various banks to inquire about possible loans. The low interest rates for female-owned small businesses made a loan a *very* attractive alternative to sinking her own savings into the shop.

Phase two called for her to research the population base in her proposed Area of Operations. Since the AO incorporated the fifty-mile stretch between Pensacola and Fort Walton Beach, Andi visited a half dozen chambers of commerce. Those helpful agencies provided a wealth of data, as did the retail merchants' associations. Andi then hit the Public Affairs folks at Eglin Air Force Base, Hurlburt Field, Pensacola Naval Air Station and nearby Whiting Field for a detailed breakdown on the ratio of military to civilian.

By the time she moved into phase three, Operation Bookstore had taken on a life of its own. Caught up in the fun and wealth of data she was amassing, Andi scoped out the local booksellers. The town of Mary Esther, adjacent to Hurlburt Field, had a small Borders Express and several used bookstores, but the closest major chain was more than thirty miles away, in Sandestin. Confident she could attract a customer base, she plunged into phase four.

As August rolled into September, she investigated what she would need in terms of business permits and tax ID numbers. That done, she checked out every strip mall in her AO.

She didn't intend to commit to a shop. Not for some time yet. But she found the perfect location less than five miles from her rented house, right there in Gulf Springs. A scuba-and-dive operation was moving to a larger facility and would vacate its present premises at the end of the week.

"I've had several inquiries about this property," the leasing agent told her as they strolled down aisles of tanks, fins and snorkel masks. "It won't remain vacant for long."

Andi knew a sales pitch when she heard one, but her gut told her the man was right. Gulf Springs occupied the westernmost tip of Santa Rosa Island, just across the Inland Waterway from Hurlburt, and had retained its small-town feel despite developers' efforts to turn it into the next hot vacation spot. Condos were springing up like sea oats along the beach east of town, along with restaurants and touristy souvenir shops.

The dive shop sat amid a cluster of oceanfront businesses. Two restaurants and several beach-type shops drew the vacation crowd. The deli, drugstore and busy video rental pulled in the locals.

Andi stood on the sidewalk outside the shop, took another look around and sucked in a deep breath.

"You've got yourself a new tenant, Mr. Jacobs."

"Great! Let's go back to my office and we'll draw up a lease agreement."

SHE PUT DOWN A DEPOSIT on Tuesday. The following Saturday she invited Sue Ellen to swing by for a guided tour. They met the leasing agent on the sidewalk outside the former scuba-and-dive shop.

"The interior needs work," Wayne Jacobs warned as he unlocked the front door. "The previous occupant moved out yesterday and left things in kind of a mess."

"*Kind* of a mess?" Sue Ellen gasped, halting just inside the threshold.

Beside her, Andi swept a dismayed gaze from the trash littering the floor to the holes punched in the drywall to the fluorescent light fixture hanging by a thin wire.

"I have a repair crew coming in tomorrow," Jacobs assured her. "They'll install new drywall, fix the floor, replace the acoustical tiles, give everything a fresh coat of paint. You won't recognize the place."

"I'd better not." She took another sweeping look around. "I expect a full refund of my deposit if you don't bring everything up to code."

"Not to worry." The agent swiped a palm over the few strands of hair covering the top of his head. "The town's building inspector is a son of a gun to work with, but I guarantee we'll meet or exceed requirements."

Once outside, Andi shrugged off her dismay and insisted on buying Sue Ellen dinner at the seafood restaurant across the street. Cap'n Sam's decor ran to fishnet, plastic seashells and picnic-bench-style tables. But the latched-back shutters gave a glorious view of the gulf, and the grilled red snapper melted in Andi's mouth. She'd taken only a few bites when a shout boomed out.

"Hey, Colonel!"

The call came from the bar, where six or seven men had gathered to wait for a table. One of them broke away from the group and vectored straight for Andi.

Heads turned. Forks stilled. Sue Ellen just about choked on her snapper. Eyes wide, she gaped at the Adonis headed their way. With his short-cropped curly hair and superbly conditioned athlete's body, he might have modeled for any of the statues adorning ancient Olympia.

"Who *is* that?"

"Major Bill Steadman." Andi's lips curved. "'Crash' to his friends."

"Any friend of yours," S.E. murmured, her gaze riveted on the heart-stopping young major, "should most definitely become one of mine."

Andi pushed back her chair and was immediately swept into a fierce bear hug. Since she and Crash were both in civilian dress, military protocol didn't stand a chance. Not after the months they'd spent working a classified project in the Nevada desert.

He set her on her feet, his handsome face alight with pleasure. "I didn't know you'd been transferred to Florida. When did you get here? What outfit are you with?"

Andi glanced at the faces turned their way. The explanation came hard with so many strangers listening in. Pinning on a breezy smile, she gave him a modified version of events. "I wasn't transferred. I put in my papers and bailed."

"The hell you say!"

"It's true. You're looking at a woman of leisure."

"Damn, Colonel." He struggled with his surprise and shock. "You would've been our first female four-star general. Everyone said so."

"Not likely," Andi countered, laughing at the absurdity of his prediction. "You know darn well any rank beyond captain is a crapshoot. What are *you* doing here?"

"I'm at Whiting Field, on a special assignment as an instructor at the Navy helicopter school."

"Uh-oh. Do they know how you earned your nickname?"

"No, and I'm not about to tell them."

His gaze slid past Andi, prompting her to make belated introductions.

"Crash, this is my friend Sue Ellen Carson. She's civil service, but don't hold that against her."

"Good to meet you, ma'am."

His respectful *ma'am* took some of the sparkle from S.E.'s smile, but she recovered swiftly and gestured to the empty places at their wooden picnic table. "You and your friends are welcome to join us."

"You might want to think about that," Crash said with a grin. "They're Navy."

"That's okay. I'm nondenominational."

He gave a crack of laughter and signaled his buddies. "Gentlemen, I'd like you to meet Ms. Sue Ellen Carson and Colonel Andrea Armstrong, the meanest, toughest, most pigheaded boss I ever worked for."

"High praise indeed," Andi drawled, "coming from the meanest, toughest, most pigheaded subordinate who ever worked for me."

Introductions made and handshakes exchanged, the group hunkered down on the benches.

Several rounds of drinks, four heaping baskets of hush puppies and mounds of fried fish later, they were still there. They would have stayed even longer if Andi hadn't called a halt to the improbable war stories and rowdy one-upmanship all helo pilots indulged in whenever they got within fifty yards of each other.

"Sorry, troops. Some of us have to work tomorrow."

"I don't," Sue Ellen protested. "Tomorrow's Sunday, remember?"

"You civil service weenies may take weekends off. Entrepreneurs like me keep our noses to the grindstone 24-7."

"You'll have to zap me an e-mail when you fix a date

for your grand opening," Crash said as he and his friends escorted the women to their car. "I'll round up the entire squadron and march them over."

"Great. I promise to stock up on Tom Clancys and W.E.B. Griffins for the occasion."

"We might even arrange a flyover," he volunteered. "One of our training routes takes us close to Stone Beach, at the southern tip of Santa Rosa Island."

"Surprise, surprise," Sue Ellen snorted. "That's the nude beach," she added at Andi's blank look.

S.E.'s gaze stayed on Crash as Andi backed the Tahoe out of its parking spot.

"That boy could fly over my southern tip anytime. Is he married?"

"He was. His wife died in a boating accident a few years back."

"Oh, no. How did he take it?"

"Hard."

Sue Ellen thought about that for a few moments before adding a casual comment. "Why don't you invite him over for dinner some evening?"

"I will now that I know he's here."

"Good. How about Tuesday? I'll bring dessert."

"Sorry, I can't do Tuesday. I'm driving up to Tennessee to meet with a book distributor and tour his warehouse.

I plan to stay overnight and probably won't get back until late Wednesday."

"Thursday, then."

Andi slanted her friend a quick glance. "You don't think Crash might be a little young for you?"

"Honey chile, the older I gets, the younger I likes 'em."

"All right, I'll invite him over. Just don't come whining to me about sagging boobs and belly flab when he gets you naked."

"My boobs do *not* sag. As for belly flab…" S.E. patted her flat, tight tummy. "Why do you think I got this diamond winkie? A little distraction goes a long way, girl."

PHASE FIVE OF Operation Bookstore required Andi to firm up arrangements with a distributor to supply her shop. Accordingly, she set out for Tennessee at oh-dark-thirty Tuesday morning.

She could have dealt with the distributor's regional rep in Florida but wanted to get a feel for the company's overall operation. Besides, except for scouting trips to Pensacola and Panama City, she hadn't been out of the immediate area since she arrived.

Leaving the Gulf coast behind her, she shot straight north through Alabama's flat fields and spindly pines. Il

Divo belted from the Tahoe's four speakers. Coffee and a couple of McDonald's breaks kept her fueled. Eager anticipation made the eight-hour trip whiz by.

Funny, she thought as she sped along I-24 toward Nashville. She'd once commanded a wing with an annual operating budget of more than three hundred million dollars. In her last job as director of operations for J-1, she'd managed joint billets scattered throughout the world.

Yet here she was, as excited about establishing an operation that probably would employ one, maybe two people and run to no more than forty thousand a year as she'd been over any of her military responsibilities.

"Everything's relative," she reminded the grinning face in the Tahoe's rearview mirror.

And this baby was hers. All hers. No boss to answer to. No large staff to encourage and support and harass. No lives affected by her decisions except her own.

She couldn't believe how good it felt. How good *she* felt. Breaking into song, she joined Il Divo in a loud, enthusiastic rendition of "Unchained Melody."

ANDI TIMED HER ARRIVAL at the distribution center outside LaVergne perfectly. After signing in at the front desk, she was escorted to the Customer Relations area and introduced to the rep who would manage her account.

A genial good old boy with a comfortable paunch and more than thirty years in the book business, Ed Saunders had prepared an info packet with enough charts, fact sheets and trend analyses to satisfy even Andi's analytical soul. They spent more than an hour discussing various discount schedules, payment options and regional readership trends. After demonstrating the company's online ordering and inventory system, Saunders led her to a golf cart for a tour of the warehouse.

"This is only one of our five regional warehouses."

Wheeling out of the lot, they putt-putted from the administrative building toward a massive windowless structure that seemed to stretch for miles.

"If you request an expedited shipment of a certain title and we're out of stock here in LaVergne, our computers will automatically ship it from the next closest center."

Andi soaked in every word like a sponge, scribbling notes when necessary on the fact sheets Saunders had provided. Her pen skittered to a halt once inside the warehouse, however.

"Good Lord!"

Grinning, the account manager looped a wrist over the golf cart's steering wheel. "We get that reaction a lot from first timers."

Awestruck, Andi took in acre upon acre of industrial

shelving stacked almost thirty feet high. The shelves were crammed with boxes bearing the labels of every publisher in the business. Forklifts chugged up and down the wide aisles ferrying pallets of more boxes. Metal bins rattled along an overhead set of tracks, whisking individual orders to the packing and shipping center.

While Saunders drove the main aisle, Andi breathed in the musty scent of cardboard and ink flavored with the stink of diesel fumes from the semis backed up to the long row of bay doors at the far end of the warehouse. Craning her neck, she almost fell out of the golf cart in an effort to take in the towers of boxed books on either side.

"This is one of the stations where we prepare individual shipments," he said, pulling up at a long counter stacked with piles of books, CDs, tapes and magazines.

They climbed out of the cart and shook hands with the "picker" working that station. As the woman explained her process for filling orders, Andi spotted a new hardcover by one of her favorite authors. She trained the tip of her finger over the cover. A thrill of sheer delight danced up and down her spine.

She felt as though she'd died and gone to book heaven.

CHAPTER 5

"You should have seen that place!"

Still jazzed from her trip to Tennessee, Andi wielded a set of salad tongs like a baton. Fresh spinach, walnuts, mandarin oranges and red onion rings flew from the serving bowl to colorful plastic salad plates.

"They maintain an inventory of over a million titles. I was swimming in the printed word."

Sue Ellen and Crash exchanged amused glances. They'd been hearing about the Great Book Expedition since they'd arrived a half hour ago. Hooking one sandaled foot under her, S.E. rocked her high-backed patio chair to the rhythm of her friend's bubbling enthusiasm.

Andi had set the table on the raised deck that angled along the side and rear of her rented house. Fine mesh screening completely enclosed the deck. Miniature lights threaded through the overhead supports gave it a romantic glow. While dog flies and skeeters buzzed outside the screens, the narrow wedge of sea visible through the dunes had slowly darkened from turquoise to cobalt to midnight-blue.

Sue Ellen loved both the deck and the view…which included Major Bill Steadman. He was sprawled in the chair next to hers, one knee hooked over the other, his red knit polo shirt tucked into khaki shorts. Sue Ellen ran her gaze over his curly hair, wide shoulders and muscular calves before forcing her attention back to her friend.

This was the Andi she'd always known. Lively, animated, her green eyes alive with plans and schemes. Any reservations Sue Ellen had harbored about Operation Bookstore had melted away.

"Their software is so easy to use," Andi was saying. "I can order by individual title, by author or by house. I can also adapt it easily to the scanning software I've been looking into."

Interrupting her dialogue, she poised the tongs over a small side bowl.

"Anyone *not* want Hungarian goat cheese on their salad? It's pretty potent."

Crash didn't hesitate. "I'm in."

Sue Ellen let her gaze roam his sculpted features again, sighed and nodded.

"Me, too."

Between the raw onions, the goat cheese and the

garlic bread toasting in the oven, she figured she wouldn't be getting up close and personal with the major tonight. There was always tomorrow, however.

Piling on the crumbly cheese, Andi picked up her narrative. "I've ordered the shelving for my store. As soon as it's set up, I'll re-verify my calculations on shelf space and send in my start-up order."

"What are you calling the store?" Crash wanted to know.

Andi made a face. As Sue Ellen knew, that was the one tab in her notebook giving her friend the most grief.

"I can't decide. I've considered and rejected hundreds of names." Sighing, she passed the salad plates. "I have to settle on one and get it to the sign maker next week, though, or my TPFD will slip."

Crash hooked a brow. "You laid out a time-phased force deployment?"

"Of course. I couldn't go into something like this without a detailed plan."

Chuckling, he stabbed at his spinach. "Looks like you can take the woman out of the military, but it doesn't work the other way around."

He was only teasing. Andi hadn't told him that her sudden retirement wasn't entirely her idea. Nor, Sue Ellen knew, did she intend to. Still, her friend had to work to return a flip response.

"Guess not."

Sympathy flashed in Sue Ellen's china-blue eyes. Deftly she steered the conversation away from hidden shoals.

"Maybe we can help you with this name business. Do you still intend to focus primarily on romance novels and thrillers?"

"Unless my analyses are completely off, that's what my customers will want."

"Hmm…let's think about this." Propping her elbows on the table, she dangled her fork between her fingers. "We're talking love and intrigue. Bedrooms and bodies. Murder and mischief."

Crash followed her lead. "How about Danger and Desire?"

"Good but a little too generic. How about Deception and Delight?"

"Good but too froufrou-y." Caught up in the game, he grinned and leaned forward. "Lust and Lies?"

"Ugh." Sue Ellen's nose wrinkled. "You just described my second husband."

"Sex and Spies?"

"Orgasms and Operatives?"

"Guns and Roses?"

Salads forgotten, they tossed possibilities back and forth. Andi followed the action, feeling more like a spectator at Wimbledon than a top-seeded player. After several more volleys, S.E. finally stumbled.

"Passion and, uh, Peril."

"Peril?" Crash hooted. "Who uses *peril* anymore?"

"Okay, wise guy. How about Under the Covers with an Undercover Agent?"

"Too long. Why don't we just go Under the Covers?"

Batting her lashes, S.E. pounced. "Your place or mine, sweetiekins?"

Her throaty purr pulled Crash up short. He blinked, obviously trying to figure out how the air had taken on such a sudden charge.

Andi could have enlightened him but decided she'd better direct the conversation back to safer ground. "I like the covers angle," she said hastily. "Book covers, bedcovers, undercover operatives. They all sort of tie together."

A lazy drawl sounded from just outside the screens. "Sounds like an interesting combination."

Sue Ellen jumped half out of her chair. Crash whirled his around. Andi merely gulped as her ex-husband moved out of the shadows and into the light.

No wonder they hadn't spotted him crossing the short distance between the two houses! He wore his jungle BDUs and boots and had a floppy-brimmed boonie hat pulled low on his forehead. Camouflage paint streaked the lower portion of his face.

"Sorry. Didn't mean to startle you."

The whites of his eyes were all that were visible as they swept over Sue Ellen and lingered on Crash for a moment before shifting back to Andi.

"I saw the lights and thought I'd come over to find out how you're doing."

"I'm fine." She rushed on, not wanting the curse to intrude on her evening. "Did you just get home?"

"Yeah, a few minutes ago."

The rusty note of weariness in his voice tugged at something deep inside Andi, something she'd thought long dead.

God! How many times had one of them dragged home after a deployment or temporary duty and unlocked the door to an empty house? How often had they eaten alone, feet propped on the coffee table in the den?

Too often, she thought with a regret that sliced bone deep. Tonight at least they could share a meal, sitting down, with friends. *Like* friends, she amended, pushing open the screen door.

"Have you had dinner?"

"Not yet."

"Want to join us? It's nothing fancy. Just salad, rice and shrimp."

"Sounds good, but I'd better go back to my place and take a quick shower first."

"Go ahead. We'll wait."

When he melted into the night, Andi let the screen door pop shut and turned to find two very different expressions on her guests' faces. Sue Ellen's brows had lifted in surprise, Crash's in curiosity. His unspoken question was easier to answer.

"That's my neighbor...and, uh, ex-husband."

Crash's jaw sagged. "That's Colonel Dave Armstrong? The man you mentioned once the entire time I worked for you—and then in somewhat less-than-flattering terms?"

Okay, maybe not so easy to answer.

"That's him."

"He lives next door?"

Grimacing, Andi jerked her chin toward the woman now shrinking down in her chair. "I have Ms. Carson here to thank for that. She somehow forgot to inform me of my neighbor's identity before I rented this place."

Sue Ellen's only defense was a weak smile. Andi let her friend squirm for a moment or two before she pushed back her chair.

"You two entertain yourselves for a few minutes. I'll get another plate and check on the shrimp."

Her departure produced a small silence. Frowning, Crash broke it after a moment or two.

"I didn't meet Andi until some years after her divorce. She didn't talk about it or her ex, but I got the impression she was still hurting."

"Divorce is never easy. Trust me on this. I know whereof I speak."

He leaned back in his chair and studied Sue Ellen through those ridiculously long lashes. They were the same shade of bronze as his short, curly hair but tipped with gold at the end.

Really, the man had no business being so gorgeous.

Or so damned young.

"You mentioned a second husband," he commented. "How many have you had?"

"Just the two. One Air Force, one civilian, both complete jerks."

She hesitated, reluctant to open an old wound. Yet his question led naturally to a follow-on.

"Andi told me you lost your wife a few years ago."

"Yeah, I did."

"I'm sorry."

The lashes came down, shielding his eyes. Sue Ellen scratched his deceased wife from the conversational list and fished for another topic.

"So how do you like working with the Navy? Honestly."

"Honestly?" He raised his head. A smile worked its way into his eyes. "It's like being dropped butt-first into a vat of brine."

"That bad, huh?"

"No, not really. They're good troops and damn good helo pilots. They do talk a different language, though. I can interpret most of the aviation slang, but I'll admit it took a while to decipher *hingehead*."

"Okay, I'll bite. What's a hingehead?"

"Me, as it turns out. That's their term for a major. Lieutenant commander, in Navy parlance. Evidently when you make 0-4, you get a lobotomy and lose half your brain. Or, in some cases, all of it. But they install a hinge so the gray matter can be reinserted later."

"Ouch. I don't think I want to hear their term for civil servants."

"No, you don't."

Their laughter greeted Andi when she returned with another place setting of the colorful plastic dinnerware she'd purchased for this occasion. Dave reappeared as she was arranging it on an equally splashy straw place mat.

"That was quick," Sue Ellen commented.

"Special Tactics never messes around when it comes to food," Andi said, trying her damnedest to ignore the water glistening on his still-damp hair and the muscled calves left bare by his cargo shorts.

"Dave, this is Bill Steadman, aka Crash. We worked a special project together at Kirtland. He's now at Whiting Field, attempting to teach Navy pilots how to fly in both the vertical and horizontal planes."

"A helo driver, huh? Is your background rescue or Special Ops?"

"Mostly rescue."

The two men indulged in that particular male ritual of crunching each other's metacarpals without appearing to exert an ounce of pressure.

When they settled at the table, the conversation revolved around the military helicopter community through most of the salad. The leafy spinach and goat cheese had all but disappeared by the time Dave recalled the discussion he'd interrupted with his sudden appearance.

"What was all that talk about book covers, bedcovers and undercover agents?"

"Sue Ellen and Crash were trying to help me come up with a name for the bookstore."

"What bookstore?"

"My bookstore. I've decided to open one."

His brows snapped together. Lowering his fork, he shot Sue Ellen a frown before pinning Andi with a hard glance.

"When did you decide that?"

"A few weeks ago."

Not, she wanted to add, that it was any of his business. For the sake of harmony, she bit back the tart comment.

Dave wasn't as restrained. "Dammit, Andi, the docs said you were supposed to take things easy."

"I am."

"By starting up a business?"

"Back off, Armstrong."

Her eyes flashed a warning Dave couldn't ignore. His mouth clamped shut with an audible click. Andi waited a beat before turning to Crash.

"Want to help me in the kitchen?"

Jaw tight, Dave's eyes followed the other two as they exited the deck. His expression was distinctly unhappy when he turned to Sue Ellen.

"Don't glower at me like that," she said testily. "I tried to talk her out of it."

"Obviously you didn't try hard enough."

"You know Andi. It takes a Sidewinder missile to knock her off course once she's locked on."

"Yeah, well, looks like I need to launch one."

"No, you don't!"

Their temporary alliance cracked and split right down the middle. Sue Ellen might stand a foot shorter and weigh a hundred pounds less than Dave Armstrong, but she could bristle like a pit bull in defense of her friend.

"You've been off slogging through swamps and barbecuing rattlesnakes. You didn't see how down Andi got. Or how restless."

"You were supposed to keep her upbeat and cheerful until I returned."

"Maybe if you tried sticking around once in a while, Armstrong, other folks wouldn't have to step in and perform that duty for you."

His mouth went white at the corners.

Sue Ellen didn't rescind the harsh criticism, but she did feel a twinge of shame at the low hit. She knew Dave had taken the divorce as hard as Andi. Harder, maybe, since he'd resisted calling it quits for so long. Reluctantly she declared a truce.

"It took me a while, but I've come around to this bookstore idea. Andi's so excited about it. And she's going at it in slow, methodical steps. Or was, until she signed the lease. You should see the three-ring binder she's put together. That sucker is five inches thick."

The frost in his blue eyes thawed a little. Not much but enough for Sue Ellen to breathe normally again. When Dave Armstrong flashed that cold laser stare, he could be just a little intimidating.

"Andi put a similar plan together for our wedding," he admitted. "Would you believe she drafted individual indexes for my parents and hers? She even laid out a timeline for our honeymoon."

"Which I suspect went out the window the minute you got her to yourself."

"As a matter of fact…"

His expression went inward, as if he were reliving

memories. X-rated memories, judging by his small, private smile.

Sue Ellen's prickly animosity faded. She didn't want to like the man, still less feel sympathy for him. Her loyalty lay squarely with Andi. Yet she had to acknowledge Dave had his former wife's best interests at heart.

"Please," she pleaded. "Don't do your colonel thing and bark or growl or issue ultimatums. Just talk to Andi about the bookstore. I'm beginning to think it could be just what the doctor ordered. What's more," she added, playing her trump card, "it will keep her in Florida. The more time and money she invests in this project, the less she's likely to pack up and leave us."

That struck a nerve. Dave drummed his fingers on the table for a few moments, considering what she'd just said. Then his thoughts winged in an entirely different direction.

"What's with Andi and this guy Steadman?"

"They're just friends."

"Christ, Andi. I thought we were supposed to be friends."

Unaware he'd echoed Sue Ellen's blithe description of their relationship, Crash glared at Andi through the steam rising from a pot of spicy Creole shrimp.

"We are."

"Then why didn't you tell me about the medical evaluation board when we bumped into each other at Cap'n Sam's the other night?"

Andi stirred the shrimp, thoroughly pissed at Dave for outing her. After his caustic comments, she'd had no choice but to explain the real impetus behind her abrupt departure from active duty.

"There was no reason to tell you about it," she said, wielding a long-handled spoon. "It's no big deal."

"Yeah, right. Just big enough to put you out of the Air Force."

"I'd been thinking about hanging up my uniform anyway."

"Since when? Last I heard, you were single-handedly reorganizing the Joint Chiefs of Staff. You were also up for BG."

"Making brigadier general isn't the end all and be all in life."

"Maybe not, but those stars were yours for the asking."

His handsome face was carved into lines of worry and frustration on her behalf. Touched, Andi set aside the spoon and laid her hand on his forearm.

"Let it go, Crash. I have."

"Have you? Really?"

She couldn't keep up the front in the face of his genuine concern. Sighing, she admitted the truth.

"Okay, I'm human. I can't *entirely* erase those sneaky thoughts about what might have been."

She'd worked so hard, given so much of herself to the Air Force. Even more after the divorce. The sixteen-hour days had numbed the worst of her aching regret and loneliness.

"I'm getting better at erasing every day, though. This bookstore is helping. I haven't felt this jazzed about a project in a long time. It's given me a reason to get up in the morning, something to look forward to."

To Andi's profound disgust, a wobble had crept into her reply. Crash responded with a curse and came around the counter.

"Christ, I'm sorry." Curling an arm around her shoulders, he gave them a friendly squeeze. "Here I am harping about the past when I should be sharing your excitement over your bright new future."

"Mmm." She sniffed, mortified by her near descent into tears. "It is exciting."

"I want an engraved invitation to the grand opening."

"Count on it," Andi said as the door to the deck slid back on its runner.

From the circle of Crash's arms she spotted Dave standing frozen in the doorway, looking very much as though he'd just been goosed with a cattle prod.

CHAPTER 6

Dave strode into the command section of the 720th Special Tactics Group at six-twenty the next morning. His BDUs were knife-creased, his pant legs neatly bloused and his mood as black as the polish on his boots.

Despite the hour, his executive officer had beat him in and had the coffee perking. A sharp young captain who'd earned his gray beret as leader of a combat weather team, Kevin Acker popped to attention at his boss's entrance.

"Morning, sir. Welcome back."

Dave grunted and made for the coffee. Mug in one hand and his bulging, much-worn leather briefcase in the other, he cut toward his office.

Acker followed with what Dave termed his "morning file." The folder contained the Early Bird—a compilation of U.S. and international news clippings faxed from the Pentagon every morning—and the classified intelligence summary of the previous twenty-four hours.

"How did the joint exercise go?" the captain asked,

placing the file squarely between the other folders arranged in precise stacks on Dave's desk. Acker had some sort of office feng shui thing going.

"Like most of 'em do," Dave bit out. "One Charlie Foxtrot after another."

Acker took the hint. His boss was in no mood for chatter. After reminding Dave he had stand-up with the wing commander at seven and a debrief with the three-star AFSOC commander at nine, the captain beat a hasty retreat.

Dave deposited his coffee mug on the brass shell fragment that served as both coaster and constant reminder of his unit's mission and tossed his maroon beret onto the credenza behind his desk.

Unlike the cubbyholes occupied by colonels at the Pentagon, offices at field headquarters tended to be bigger, better furnished and more in keeping with the responsibilities that came with commanding an elite force of warriors. Dave's measured a good thirty by forty, with plenty of room for a double pedestal desk and credenza in dark mahogany, a high-backed executive chair, a conference table large enough for his twelve-person senior staff to gather around and a seating group that included a man-size leather sofa, two easy chairs and a coffee table.

He'd chosen not to put up an I-love-me display of the plaques, awards and military memorabilia he'd collected over the years. Instead he'd instructed his exec to hang black-and-white photos of Special Tactics forces in action. Before Dave made any decision, he'd skim a glance around the gallery. His troops' grim, determined faces usually clarified even the most complicated issues.

Judging by the stacks of folders on his desk, he was looking at plenty of tough issues today. He took another swig of coffee, flipped open the intelligence summary and tried to bend his mind around events that had happened in every corner of the globe in the past twenty-four hours.

An event *not* included in the summary kept sabotaging his concentration. Dave tried to put last night out of his mind. Swilled more coffee. Glared at the printed pages. Despite his best efforts, he couldn't blank out the image of Andi cuddled up against another man's chest.

Finally he abandoned the pretense of even trying. Mouth tight, he lifted his phone and stabbed the intercom button.

Acker answered immediately. "Yes, sir?"

"Get me a personnel rip on a major by the name of Bill Steadman. He's an Air Force helo driver, currently assigned as an instructor at Whiting Field."

"Yes, sir."

AS DAVE'S DAY PROGRESSED, it went from bad to pure crap. Meetings ate up the whole morning. Afternoon brought the grim news that a Special Ops C-130 crashed on takeoff from Kadena Air Force Base, Japan.

Everyone on board walked away, thank God, but the aircraft sustained considerable damage. Dave was tasked to provide representatives for both the Safety Investigation Board being assembled immediately and the Accident Investigation Board to follow.

It was past seven when he departed the base that evening. The tall long-leaf pines crowding U.S. 98 threw pointed shadows across the road. Once over the Navarre Bridge, a soft September dusk painted the dunes with purple shadows and the sea a deep, dark indigo.

Dave was in no mood to appreciate either the view or the balmy seventy-two-degree temperature. Fourteen- and sixteen-hour days were nothing new, but this one sat like a rock on his shoulders. The personnel data he'd reviewed on Major Bill Steadman hadn't exactly lightened the load.

The helo pilot had racked up a helluva record in his fourteen years of service. Air Force Academy grad, top gun from undergraduate pilot training, two combat tours, staff experience, early promotion to major. It was clear the kid was being groomed for command and top rank.

The call Dave made to a friend who'd had Steadman in his unit confirmed that impression. Harry Rockingham swore Crash was not only a highly skilled pilot and a natural leader, he was universally liked by other members of his squadron.

That "universally liked" remained lodged like a burr inside Dave's head…right along with the image of Andi falling all over Bill Steadman's chest.

It wasn't jealousy eating at him. He knew every one of Andi's moods. He'd seen her face light up with joy, her cheeks suffuse with anger, her eyes grow heavy with desire. He didn't believe for a second she'd turned to pretty boy Steadman in passion.

But she *had* turned to him for comfort. Dave had spotted the telltale sheen of tears, caught the uncharacteristic slump to her shoulders. She'd let down her guard with Steadman yet continued to shut Dave out. That pecked at his insides like a big black crow picking at roadkill.

Deciding to take the edge off his frustration with a take-out dinner from his favorite Chinese restaurant, he called ahead to order spicy Szechuan beef and noodles with a side of spring rolls. He'd picked up his order and had begun to head home when he spotted a red Tahoe with D.C. plates angled into a parking slot in front of an empty store. Slowing, Dave squinted to peer through the shop windows.

"Hell!"

Stomping on the brake pedal, he spit out a string of curses and cut the wheel.

His pickup screeched into the slot beside the Tahoe. His boots hit the pavement. Blood thundering in his ears, he slammed through the shop's front door and let loose with an enraged bellow.

"Are you out of your mind!"

His bull-like roar set off an unintended chain reaction. Andi was already overbalanced near the top of a six-foot ladder, propping a bookcase against the wall with one hand while she attempted to screw it to a brace with the other.

His shout sent her screwdriver flying. Startled, she twisted around and lost her grip on the bookshelves. The heavy case tilted. The ladder wobbled. Andi went airborne.

Leaping over scattered tools and discarded packing materials, Dave caught her just before she hit the floor. He clamped her against him, his heart battering against his ribs, and expressed himself with what he considered admirable restraint given the circumstances.

"Dammit, woman! You don't have the sense God gave a drunken duck."

"Me!"

Screeching with outrage, Andi struggled in his arms. Dave clamped them tighter.

"What in hell possessed you to go climbing ladders?"

Both his tone and his accusation infuriated Andi. She knew damn well she couldn't win a wrestling match with Dave. He'd pinned her to the mat—and to the mattress—too many times. But that didn't mean she had to take whatever he decided to dish out.

Going rigid, she flung his angry words right back at him. "What in hell possessed you to barge in and scare the crap out of me?"

"I was driving by and spotted your car. Then I spotted you."

His voice was as dangerous as broken glass. She felt every one of the sharp edges.

"Seeing you perched on that ladder scared the crap out of *me*," he ground out.

Andi had to believe him. The tendons in his neck stood out like ropes. His heart hammered so hard and fast she could feel its beat right through his uniform.

Hers wasn't exactly dragging along. Pulling in a deep breath, she made a grudging admission. "Okay, maybe climbing that ladder wasn't the smartest thing I've ever done."

"No *maybe* about it."

So much for defusing his temper! Or hers. The snide remark reignited the sparks.

"I don't need this, Armstrong. I've had an all-around rotten day."

"Tell me about it."

"Go to hell."

The rock-hard planes of his face softened. "That came out wrong. I didn't mean to sound sarcastic."

Keeping her imprisoned against his chest, he put his shoulders to the wall and slid down until his butt hit the floor. Hers hit the rock-hard planes of his belly.

"Tell me," he said, loosening his hold enough for her to wiggle into a sitting position.

Andi knew she should push out of his arms, dust off her bottom, thank him for his concern and get back to work. The memory of all the times they'd shared their worries and frustrations at work overcame common sense.

Thrusting a hand through her sweat-dampened hair, she jerked her chin toward the cartons stacked ten high against the opposite wall.

"It's these damned bookshelves. They were delivered this afternoon. Three hours late, I might add. The delivery crew was supposed to put them together."

"Why didn't they?"

"Uncrating and setup weren't included in their instructions—or so they insisted. By the time I got hold of a supervisor, it was past five and the crew was off the clock. We had to reschedule."

"So you decided not to wait?" Disapproval followed hard on the heels of disbelief. "You were going to set them up? By yourself?"

"Not all of them," she huffed, bristling again. "Just that one. I wanted to see how it looked and take the shelf measurements."

He gathered steam for another scathing remark. Andi narrowed her eyes to slits, daring him to utter it. Their silent duel lasted a good five or ten seconds until Dave bit back whatever he'd intended to say.

The effort damn near choked him. He still hadn't recovered from his stark terror at seeing her topple off the ladder. Or his fury at her for climbing up on it in the first place. Now the weight of her bottom digging into his groin was shooting what little was left of his control all to hell.

Shifting, he eased her to a less sensitive spot. "What else went wrong with your day?"

"You name it." Shoulders hunched, she deflated like a balloon. "The occupancy permit I applied for still hasn't come through. When I called the city offices this morning, I got a runaround like you wouldn't believe."

"And?"

"And the computer wiz who was supposed to come in and give me an estimate for the wireless terminals I want installed failed to show."

"Sounds like the civilian world isn't cooperating with your time-phased deployment schedule."

"No kidding," she said glumly. "If any of these folks

had been military, I would have charged them with AWOL or failure to repair."

He wanted to sympathize with her but was still hauling the weight of his own day.

"It could have been worse, Andi."

"Oh? You want to tell me how?"

"You could have fallen off that ladder and broken a few bones. Or lost a 130."

He hadn't meant to let that slip out. She had enough on her mind right now without adding his problems to her own. The media would pick up on the accident soon enough, however. Just as well she heard it from him first.

"Oh, no!" Her voice flooding with dismay, she wiggled around to face him. "When? Where?"

"This morning, at Kadena."

"What about the crew?"

"Everyone aboard walked away."

"Thank God!"

The giant fist squeezing Andi's heart eased its grip. Nothing hit an Air Force member faster or with more gut-wrenching impact than hearing a plane had gone down. It hit even harder when there was a very real possibility close friends had been aboard.

"What happened?"

"It's too early to be sure, but it looks like they encountered a vicious wind shear on takeoff and went nose-down into the runway."

He leaned back and propped his head against the wall. He looked so tired, Andi thought, yanked away from her petty problems. So different from the cocky captain who'd swooped in and swept her off her feet all those years ago.

When he'd jogged toward her on the beach recently, she'd thought he looked as strong and superbly conditioned as ever. Seeing him now, this close, this unguarded, Andi noted the subtle changes.

His tanned skin still stretched taut over his cheeks and chin, but a network of fine lines had become etched at the corners of his eyes and mouth. And was that a hint of silver threading through his coal-black hair?

It was!

"You're going gray, Armstrong."

"You just now noticing?"

Fascinated by those errant strands, she ran her fingers through the short, thick layers.

"I'm glad I'm not the only one showing signs of age."

"Now that you mention it," he said with a slow smile, "I have noticed a few wrinkles. They look good."

His glance drifted over her face and snagged at her jawline. His smile fading, he traced the small white scar with his thumb.

"This from Iraq?"

"Yes."

"I didn't learn you were in that marketplace until two days after the explosion."

She shrugged aside the implied accusation. "I wasn't hurt. All I got was this little scratch."

"And the bacteria that slipped into your blood through the open wound."

"And that."

As his calloused pad feathered over her skin, it occurred to Andi they were alone in the empty shop, nested together like Russian dolls.

The same thought must have occurred to Dave. His thumb stilled. The air seemed to get heavy around them.

Andi sensed his intent a second or two before he leaned into her. Her pulse skipping and stuttering, she splayed a hand against his chest.

"Wait, Dave."

"For what?"

"This…this isn't smart."

"Maybe not," he murmured, his mouth a mere inch or two from hers. "Then again, it could be the smartest thing we've done in years."

Andi ached to feel his mouth on hers again. So much she hurt with it. She came within a breath of dropping her hand, lifting her lips and inviting him inside the gates again. Knowing the invitation would only lead to more hurt stopped her cold.

Her life had made a sharp right turn in the past month or so, but Dave's hadn't. He was still in uniform, still living, breathing and sleeping Special Tactics. Still gone more than he was home. Andi wasn't ready to take on either the worry or the long, empty nights again.

"I can't do this. Not now. Not yet."

She'd left the door open. Intentionally or otherwise— Andi was damned if she knew which at that point. Dave acknowledged as much with a reluctant nod.

"I won't push you. Yet."

With that unsubtle warning, he lifted her off her perch and rolled to his feet. His hand was warm and strong as he tugged her up.

"Tell you what. I've got Chinese takeout in my car. How about we chow down, then I'll attach this bookcase to the wall and help you with the measurements?"

"From the sound of it, your day was a lot worse than mine. Are you sure you don't want to go home and hit the beach for a run?"

"I'm sure. We can use the packing crate as a table."

TWO HOURS LATER DAVE followed Andi's red Tahoe through the warm September night. As promised, he'd shared his spicy Szechuan beef, secured her bookcase and patiently held one end of the tape measure while she dragged the other along the shelves. All the while he'd had to fight to keep from reneging on his promise.

Andi didn't know how close he'd come to letting his gnawing hunger for her slip its leash. How close *she'd* come to being tumbled back onto a bed of cardboard packing material. If not for those unshuttered shop windows and bright, fluorescent lights...

He'd do better next time, he vowed.

Dave was close on Andi's tail when she turned onto their street. He hit the garage opener but kept his vehicle idling in his driveway until she'd pulled into hers. The fact they were going to separate garages In separate houses with separate beds ate at him like acid.

Her garage door rumbled up and the Tahoe nosed inside. Andi slid out of the vehicle, her long legs exiting first, the rest of her following a moment later. Dave was okay until she bent to reach across the driver's seat and the hem of her blouse parted company with her jeans. When a stretch of smooth, curved spine came into view, he climbed halfway out of his vehicle.

He could still feel the imprint of the hand she'd laid against his chest. Then there was the ache in his groin. He hadn't stopped hurting since Andi had landed in his lap.

The image of her overbalancing on that ladder

brought him the rest of the way out of his vehicle. His shout boomed across the adjoining drives.

"Hey, Armstrong!"

She backed out of her car with an oversize binder and a tool bag in hand. "Yes?"

"Are you going down to the shop tomorrow?"

"Yes. I've got an electrician coming in at nine to do some wiring. Why?"

"Promise me you won't uncrate any more of those bookshelves."

"I might uncrate a couple more, but I won't try to set them up."

"Dammit, Andi…"

"Night, Dave. Thanks for dinner and, well, everything."

Was that what they'd come to? he thought as she hit a switch and started the garage door rattling back down. Neighbors calling good-night across separate driveways?

Like hell!

His jaw tight, Dave flipped up his cell phone and punched in the speed-dial number for Chief Master Sergeant Joe Goodwin.

Dave and the chief went back a long way. So long that neither needed to bother with the formality of rank, although both meticulously observed it. Their respect for each other ran too deep to cross the invisible lines.

"I need a favor, Chief."

"You got it, Colonel."

His eyes locked on the house next door, Dave outlined his requirements.

"Consider it done," Goodwin said crisply.

CHAPTER 7

Sue Ellen couldn't believe her eyes!

She'd swung by the former scuba-and-dive shop on her way home from work on the off chance Andi might still be puttering around. To S.E.'s delight, she was—assisted by what looked like acres of bulging male muscle.

It came in all shapes, sizes and skin tones. Sweat glistened on bulked-up ebony shoulders. Freckles and reddish hair spackled arms the size of tree trunks, two of which were attached to the torso of a Viking hulk. A welterweight with melting brown eyes and skin the color of dark oak flexed an impressive set of pecs as he crab-walked a tall bookcase into line with two others.

Dazzled by the display, Sue Ellen almost missed Andi. She was near the back of the shop, dwarfed by a sea of discarded packing materials, feeding pieces of the industrial-strength cardboard to another hunk, who folded and compressed the thick sheets like tissue paper.

Feasting on the display, Sue Ellen wove her way through the forest of masculinity. She'd scheduled a meeting with the head of the Automotive Retailers Association in Pensacola this afternoon and had suited up for the occasion. Her silk blouse, tailored navy suit and three-inch spike heels added oomph to her five-foot-two-inch frame but didn't make for easy navigation through half-assembled shelving units.

"Hey, girlfriend."

Andi returned her greeting with a smile that showed some wear and tear at the edges. "Hey, S.E. I didn't see you come in. Did you just get here?"

"I did. If I'd known you were throwing a party for all these hotties," she added, eyeing a stud with a shaved head and a bull-like neck using a crowbar to pry open a carton, "I would have stopped by sooner."

"I didn't throw this party." The comment held a blend of amusement, exasperation and chagrin. "The chief did."

The man wielding the crowbar straightened. He was older than the others, S.E. saw, and considerably more seasoned. What she'd mistaken for a shaved head was actually grayish hair buzzed so close to his scalp as to appear nonexistent.

"Sue Ellen, this is Chief Master Sergeant Joe Goodwin. Chief, my friend Sue Ellen Carson."

He folded S.E.'s hand in a thorny paw, his smile something less than friendly. "Ms. Carson and I have met before."

"We have?"

"A few months ago, when you pulled the plug on the summer training camp I want to establish for local kids. I came to your office to discuss it."

Sue Ellen remembered him now. He looked different out of uniform, without his badges and ribbons and his beret positioned low on his forehead.

She also remembered their so-called discussion. That was the closest she'd come to losing her cool in more years than she could remember.

"There are strict guidelines for the training and employment of kids under the age of eighteen."

"Yeah, you emphasized that point. Several times."

Sue Ellen was no proponent of bureaucratic red tape. Still, there were rules and then there were rules.

"If you'd coordinated with my office *before* initiating your program, I would have reviewed it for compliance with Department of Labor regulations and sent it up my chain for approval."

"Instead you just shut me down."

"That's right, I did. Submit the proper paperwork, get up-front approval and I might reconsider."

Andi figured she'd better jump in, and fast. The chief's chin stuck out like the prow of an Antarctic icebreaker. Sue Ellen's had tipped to a dangerous angle.

"I'd better get a copy of those guidelines, too. I've had

several kids come by asking about the possibility of part-time employment."

"No problem. I'll e-mail you a copy."

The head-on collision avoided, Sue Ellen swept another look around the shop. Her glance met and mingled with one particularly prime specimen before shifting back to Andi.

"What can I do to help?"

"In those heels? Nothing."

"I'm here, I'm available. Might as well put me to work."

"Well…"

Andi brushed back the stubborn strand that had escaped her ponytail and now dangled over one eye. She had a thousand things that needed doing, not the least of which was feeding her horde of volunteers.

"The guys gave up their afternoon off to help me. I've supplied them with beer and Gatorade, but they need solid fuel to keep going."

"I can handle that. I'll hit the deli a couple doors down. Sliced ham, turkey and provolone coming right up."

"You'd better throw some red meat in there," the chief advised in a dry voice.

"Really?"

Andi tensed as the two squared off again. With her

short, feathery hair and deep purple eyes, Sue Ellen looked like a delicate porcelain doll next to the leathery chief. Just went to show how deceptive appearances could be.

"How would you like that beef?" she asked with saccharine sweetness. "Rare and bloody or still on the hoof?"

"However they want to slice it. These men are—"

Andi flung up a hand. "We know, Chief."

She knew what was coming. She'd heard it often enough. So had Sue Ellen. The two women dropped their voices several octaves and grunted in chorus.

"They're Special Tactics."

"Damn straight," Goodwin muttered.

TO ANDI'S RELIEF, JOE GOODWIN and S.E. declared a truce long enough to feed the troops. Dinner was a haphazard affair. The men consumed crusty subs layered three inches thick with minimum fuss and maximum speed. Tubs of potato salad, coleslaw and baked beans disappeared with equal efficiency. The work went on around the impromptu picnic until every tub was empty and every shelf had been screwed into place.

Andi could hardly find words to thank them. Or the chief when he pulled another huge favor out of his hat. It came in the form of a casual question.

"Are you planning to stock any books by Roger Brent?"

"A few, seeing as he's only the biggest, hottest name in

military thrillers these days. I'm hoping the sequel to *Blood Sport* will hit the stands in time for my grand opening."

"He lives in Mobile, you know."

"You're kidding."

Her mind was already leaping ahead to the possibility of convincing the *New York Times* bestselling author to drive over for an autographing. Chief Goodwin was one step ahead of her.

"Public Affairs asked me to provide technical assistance on the sequel. Brent and I got pretty close last year. You want me to give him a call, see if he might come by and sign some copies?"

"Yes!"

Visions of hordes of troops jamming into the shop for an autographed copy of the latest Roger Brent thriller filled Andi's head when she finally locked up and climbed into the Tahoe.

Darkness blocked any view of the sea but didn't muffle its soothing murmur. She sat for a moment, keys in hand, windows rolled down to let in the breeze. She ached all over, but it was a good kind of hurt, the kind that came from seeing a job completed and marking it off her checklist well ahead of schedule.

Andi knew darned well who was responsible for making that happen. Goodwin swore all he'd done was let drop a hint that Mrs. Colonel Armstrong needed a few strong backs, and volunteers had poured out of the woodwork. She'd wasted her breath reminding him she was no longer Mrs. Colonel Armstrong. To Joe Goodwin and the rest of the men who had cheerfully sacrificed their precious afternoon off, once Special Tactics, always Special Tactics.

Sighing, she dug her cell phone out of her purse and punched in the number for Dave's office. Caller ID must have tagged her, as he answered on the second ring.

"Hey, Andi. What's up?"

"My bookcases. All of them."

"They are, huh?"

"Don't play innocent. I know you sicced Joe Goodwin on me."

"Now that you mention it, I might have let slip that you could use a hand or two."

"He brought half the squadron with him."

"Did he? Good man." Dave didn't bother to hide his satisfaction. "Where are you now?"

"Getting ready to head home. You?"

"Still at work. It's been a bitch of a day."

"Tell me."

"Same old crap," he related. "Too many operational requirements, too little funding. I'm heading up to Washington next week to defend next year's budget submission to the House Armed Services Committee."

Bathed by the breeze, Andi rested her head against the seat back. Whatever else they'd screwed up in their marriage, they'd always been able to talk about their work. The sadness of that, the emptiness of it, wormed through the guilty pleasure stirred by his voice.

"How about you?" he asked after a few moments. "What's next on your checklist?"

"I've got to do battle with the city and find out what's holding up final approval of my occupancy permit."

"Anything I can do from this end?"

"You've done enough."

Raising her head, Andi shook off her lethargy. Sharing her day with Dave like this was too comfortable, too insidious. She had to be careful she didn't wind up leaning on him. She faced too many uncertainties in her life right now to add a rekindled relationship with her ex-husband to the list.

"Thanks for sending the guys over this afternoon. I really appreciate the help. But…"

She bit her lip, searching for the right words. Dave supplied them himself.

"But you want me to back off?"

"Yes. I told you last night I'm not ready to take up where we left off four years ago."

"Me, either, seeing as we left off in divorce court. If we do this again, we do it right."

"*If* being the operative word. Don't push it, Armstrong. Or me."

She was feeling cornered, Dave thought. Maybe a little confused. And he was sure he detected a touch of indecision under the irritation.

Good! He wanted to keep her off balance, give her something other than that damn bug to worry about. He didn't want her to bolt, however, or surgically remove him from her life again.

"Message received. Consider me officially backed off three paces."

"Make it ten."

"Four…five…six…seven. Sorry, babe. That's as far as I can go. You've got my ass against the wall."

She'd had his ass to the wall before. On several memorable occasions, as best Dave recalled. Her quick indrawn hiss told him the erotic images had flooded into her head as well as his. He was reliving one particularly fond memory when she cut the connection.

"Gotta go. See you around, Armstrong."

"If you're lucky, Armstrong."

FUELED BY CHEERFUL determination and a good night's sleep, Andi marched up the sidewalk to the Gulf Springs municipal center at oh-nine-hundred the following morning.

The municipal center occupied a low one-story building with giant palmettos fanning the main entrance. The offices of the town clerk shared space with the police department, the volunteer fire brigade and the library.

The locked front doors put the first dent in Andi's sunny mood. She checked her watch, folded her arms and tapped a foot. Three minutes passed. Five.

She checked her watch and tried the door again. Frowning, she skirted the palmettos. The black-and-white patrol car parked at the end of the building led her to a side door and the police department's dispatch center.

A uniformed officer manned the center. More or less. He was tipped back in his chair, feet propped on his desk, perusing a dog-eared edition of *Sportfisherman*. Andi eyed the mound of stomach straining his dark blue shirt and wondered how he managed a hot pursuit.

"Mornin', ma'am." The magazine was laid aside. His feet drifted to the floor. "What can I do for you?"

"I need to talk to the clerk who handles business permits."

"That'll be Bernice Dobbs. Just go round to the main entrance, first office to the left inside."

"I tried the main entrance. The door's locked."

His glance cut to the wall clock above the radio

console. "Should be open. Hold on, I'll… Oh, wait. This is Thursday, isn't it?"

Andi had to think a minute. The days had begun to blend together. "Yes, it is."

"Bernice goes to the vet on Thursdays."

"'Scuse me?"

"It's that yappy poodle of hers. Has a problem with its anal glands. Won't let anyone but Doc Anderson ream 'em out, but the doc only holds clinic here on Santa Rosa Island Thursday mornings."

That was considerably more information than Andi wanted or needed.

"Is there someone else I can talk to about permits?"

"Nope, just Bernice. She'll be along soon. How about a cup of coffee while you wait?"

This wasn't the Pentagon, Andi reminded herself. Zealous employees didn't come in at five or six in the morning to prepare for seven-thirty stand-up. Nor did she have a staff to delegate mundane tasks to like this one. Reining in her impatience, she accepted a mug of what looked, smelled and tasted like Alabama mud.

Ten minutes later a series of shrill yips echoed through the corridor linking the dispatch center with the city office.

"That'll be—"

"Bernice." Andi had figured that one out on her own. "Thanks for the coffee."

"Anytime." The officer's feet went back up on the console. The magazine flipped open. "We're here to serve."

Andi had always heard that dog owners often resembled their pets. Bernice Dobbs proved an exception to the rule. The poodle was small and skittish and bared its teeth when Andi walked in. Its owner was big, slow and flashed a smile that knew no strangers. Shushing her pet, Bernice ambled to the counter.

"Good morning. You're here early."

With some effort, Andi bit back the observations that *she* and her yippy pet were here late.

"My name is Andrea Armstrong. I spoke with you a couple of days ago about the occupancy permit I filed electronically with your office."

"I'm sorry, Ms. Armstrong. It's still not approved."

"What's the problem now?"

Her leasing agent had already gone two rounds with the building inspector. After the first one, Wayne Jacobs had brought in an electrician to rewire the circuitry. The second had resulted in new panic bars for the rear exit.

"The inspector indicated some of the shop's sprinkler heads aren't up to code."

"Are you sure? He didn't say anything about sprinkler heads during his first two walk-throughs."

Bernice shuffled to a computer terminal, booted up and clicked a few keys.

"Yep, that's what it was. I sent Wayne Jacobs an e-mail yesterday to let him know."

"This is ridiculous. How many walk-throughs does it take to get a business permit in this town?"

The clerk toyed with the keyboard, not quite meeting Andi's eye. "Does seem like a hassle, doesn't it?"

"Yes, it does."

Bernice worried the keys for another moment. When she lifted her gaze to Andi's again, she cocked her head and seemed to be taking her measure.

"You might want to talk to Wayne about the hassle," she said slowly.

"Why? Is he part of the problem?"

"Just talk to Wayne."

ANDI CAUGHT THE LEASING agent at his office just off Main Street. He kept a phone wedged between his neck and shoulder while his fingers flew over his computer keyboard. Smiling an apology, he waved her to a seat.

"I have just what you're looking for," he said into the phone. "Three-bedroom, two-bath, with garage, only eight miles from the base. There's another I want you to look at, too, a little farther out. I'll e-mail you both listings. I've got pictures of the interiors on my Web site. Give me a call after you've looked them over. Uh-huh. Uh-huh. Sure, I can do that. Talk to you in a little bit."

Unwedging the phone, he flipped it shut and tossed it on the desk. "I'm glad you stopped by. You were next on my call list."

"Let me guess. Sprinkler heads."

"How'd you know?"

"I just came from Bernice."

"She in already?" Surprised, he shot a glance at his watch. "She usually opens a little later on Thursdays."

"Good Lord! Does everyone in town know about her poodle's anal glands?"

His face split in a grin. He was a medium-size man with thinning strands of sandy hair and the engaging personality required to succeed as a Realtor.

"Everyone who does business with her," he confided with a chuckle.

"She said I should talk to you."

His grin faded. "I'm sorry about those damn sprinkler heads. I'll get them changed out."

"Why didn't the building inspector find them the first two times through?"

Jacobs shifted in his chair and palmed the few strands combed across his nearly bald dome. "I warned you he was a son of a gun to work with."

"Yes, you did. What's his problem?"

"It's a game he plays. Use up your patience, wear you down."

"You mean he's deliberately stonewalling us?"

"Not you. Me."

"Why?"

"Because I haven't slipped the bastard anything on the side," Jacobs admitted.

Her jaw sagged. "He wants a bribe?"

"He's never come right out and asked for one. Talbot's too damn smart to put something like that into words. But, yes, that's exactly what he wants."

"Good grief! Why don't you report him to the mayor or the town council or whoever he works for?"

"Report what?" Jacobs palmed his comb-over again. "That he's overzealous in his inspections? That he spots deficiencies on his second or third walk-through he didn't spot the first time around?"

"Gulf Springs is a small town, Wayne. If this guy is on the take, wouldn't word get around?"

"I've heard rumbles over the years, but no one will admit to offering an outright bribe. That would make them as culpable as the person accepting it. Most just write it off as a necessary cost of doing business."

"Then pass on the cost to their customers."

"And, if pressed, they'll tell you that's how it's done in the real world."

Disgusted, Andi shook her head. Bribes and under-the-table deals weren't unique to the civilian world. Just

a few years back the Pentagon's highest-ranking pro-
curement official had pleaded guilty to peddling her in-
fluence on a major aircraft buy in exchange for a
seven-figure salary when she left DOD. Yet the same
official had mandated that the troops in the trenches
couldn't accept so much as a cup of coffee from a defense
contractor.

Andi didn't believe in double standards. And she
wasn't about to launch her bookstore with a bribe.

"I don't want you to pay this guy a penny under the
table, Wayne."

"He could drag his feet indefinitely. You might have
to adjust the schedule in that notebook you tote around."

Andi suspected her notebook was fast gaining as much
local notoriety as Bernice's poodle's anal glands.

"Just let me know when this Talbot character schedules
his next walk-through. I want to be present for this one."

CHAPTER 8

Andi stewed about the permit for most of the next few days but didn't let the delay throw her too far off schedule. Wayne insisted the permit would go through one way or another. He'd also encouraged her to press ahead with the next items on her checklist.

The first was installation of the front counter she'd had rebuilt to her specifications. The carpenter delivered it along with the stands for the two used computers she'd purchased dirt cheap at a pawn shop.

That purchase prompted a call to the computer wiz recommended by Sue Ellen. The kid could write programs in his sleep—or so S.E. swore. The high schooler bopped into the shop after school sporting rings in both nostrils and baggy pants that showed most of his butt crack.

Despite Andi's initial doubts, he took less than an hour to install and integrate the bar-code-scanning software she'd purchased. Now prospective customers could go to either terminal, click a button and search her entire in-store inventory—when she ordered it. She wasn't about to ship in thousands of dollars' worth of books until her permit came through.

But she *could* bring in a few pieces of furniture. She had a sofa and two overstuffed easy chairs in storage. They didn't do her any good sitting in the rented climate-controlled unit. She might as well put them to work in her shop. When and if she moved into a permanent residence, she'd treat herself to new ones.

The sofa she placed near the front of the store, out of the glare of the sun from the plate glass windows but with enough natural light for customers to sit and read comfortably. The easy chairs fit into a spacious niche between the bookshelves designed for just that purpose.

Several potted palms and a leafy ficus added to the ambience, as would the bestseller covers Andi planned to enlarge to poster size. She'd purchased precut sheets of Plexiglas to use for mounting. Since she intended to change the displays often, she'd left the left edge of the Plexiglas open so she could slide the covers in and out easily. The other edges she would screw to the walls.

Her cell phone pinged while she was deciding where to mount the first square. The digital readout tagged the caller as Mary Esther Signs and Banners.

"Your shop sign is ready, Ms. Armstrong. When do you want us to bring it out?"

Today! Andi wanted to shout. *Right now!*

Swallowing her frustration, she scheduled the installation for the following week. No sooner had she terminated that call than she got another.

"Sorry it took me so long to get back to you," Chief Goodwin said. "Roger Brent's been out of town and just returned my call."

With so many tasks occupying her mind, Andi had almost forgotten Goodwin's promise to contact the *New York Times* bestselling author.

"Brent wants to know when your grand opening is. He might be able to swing by to sign books."

Andi's frustration made another sharp spike. "I haven't set the date yet."

"No problem. Brent said I should give you his e-mail address so you can coordinate with him directly. He also said he might be able to get his publisher to run some promo spots on radio and TV. Ready to copy?"

She snatched up a pen. "Ready."

When Goodwin reeled off the address, Andi thanked him once again. "I owe you for this, Joe. Big-time. You'll have to tell me how I can return the favor."

"If I'm in the field when Brent swings by, you might save me an autographed copy. You might also talk to your friend at the Department of Labor and tell her to cut me some slack on my youth camp."

"You got it."

The back-to-back calls spurred Andi to direct action. Determined to bring the matter of her permit to a head, she punched in a speed-dial number.

"Wayne, it's Andi. I need this guy Talbot to get off his butt and schedule another walk-through."

"I'm on the other line with him right now. Hold on."

Tapping an impatient foot, she skimmed a glance around the shop. The empty shelves stood like silent sentinels, begging to be filled. The sofa cushions were plumped and ready. The computer terminals needed only the touch of a finger to blink awake.

Andi couldn't believe how much of herself she'd already put into the bookstore. Or how eager she was to invest more. Not just money or hardware or furniture. This small shop in this little town was anchoring her in a way she'd never expected or experienced.

She'd moved more times than she could count, first as a military brat, then as an officer. As best Andi could recall, she'd never lived anywhere longer than three years. Most places it was less than two. Even this move to Florida had been intended as a stopgap measure while she battled her vicious little bug and figured out what she wanted to do with the rest of her life.

She'd decided to open her shop as a stopgap, more something to occupy her time and direct her energies than a long-term career choice. Until this moment, she hadn't thought beyond the grand opening.

Yet now, with half of the pieces coming together, she couldn't wait to get on with the rest. She wanted to watch her ideas take root. See her brainchild grow. Find out if she had as good a head for the private sector as she had for the military.

The shop had become much more than a stopgap, she realized. It was part of her.

"Okay," Jacobs said, coming back on the line. "We're on for two o'clock tomorrow."

"Good! I'll be here."

"You sure? Might be better if I handled this alone."

"I'll be here."

She hung up, thinking fast. The shop's security system didn't include high-tech surveillance cameras, but Andi knew just where to get her hands on one. The minicamcorder had been state-of-the-art when she'd bought it years ago and was probably five or six generations out of date now. No matter. Its miniature size and powerful microphone would serve her purposes perfectly.

Trying to remember when Dave had said he was leaving for D.C., Andi flipped her phone open again and dialed information. Two minutes later, she was connected to the 720th Special Tactics Group headquarters.

"This is the 720th commander's office, Captain Acker speaking."

"This is…"

Andi hesitated. She was entitled to use her military rank. God knew she'd earned it. Still, it made for an awkward conversation in situations like this one.

With a mental shrug, she identified herself. "This is Colonel Andrea Armstrong. Is the other Colonel Armstrong available?"

"Hold on, ma'am. I'll see if he's in."

Now there was a well-trained exec, Andi thought wryly. Never put an ex-wife through without checking with the boss first.

Dave picked up a few moments later, his voice sharp with concern. "Andi? You okay?"

Hell! She should have realized a call from her would trigger this kind of reaction. It wasn't as if she contacted him regularly. Or often.

"I'm fine. I just wondered if you still have that minicamcorder I gave you our last Christmas together."

"Yeah, somewhere."

"Can I borrow it?"

"Sure."

"Give me a call when you get home tonight. I'll pop over and pick it up."

"Will do."

SHE WAS ATTACHING THE last Plexiglas square to the wall behind her shiny, freshly refinished counter when her cell phone chimed again.

"I'm home," Dave announced.

"Already? You working civilian hours now, Armstrong?"

"Guess so. The moon's barely up."

"Huh?"

Swiveling, Andi saw with some shock that the shop windows had gone dark. What had happened to the afternoon?

"I don't see any lights in your windows," Dave commented. "Where are you?"

"Still at the bookstore."

"Jesus, Andi. It's almost nine. Have you been there all day?"

"No."

She wasn't lying, only stretching facts a tad. She'd run over to the copy shop across the street to enlarge a sample book cover and test it in the first wall mounting. The process had consumed all of fifteen minutes, but she didn't figure that was any of Dave's business.

"I'm leaving now. Be home shortly."

She should have run out for more than posters, Andi realized when she bent to replace her drill and screwdriver in her tool bag.

Black spots danced in front of her eyes. When the

spots blurred into a wave of dizziness, Andi slapped a hand against the counter to steady herself.

Her first panicky thought was that she'd overstressed her heart. Her second chased away the panic.

She hadn't *over*done it. She'd *under*done it.

Like a fool, she'd worked straight through lunch and dinner. She'd plug this sinking sensation on the way back to the house.

That was the plan, anyway. She might have stuck to it, too, if Crash hadn't called just after she pulled out of the drive-through lane of Hardee's. Her broiled chicken sandwich and curly fries remained in their bag while Andi cruised toward home and brought Bill up to speed on events at the store.

"That would be a real coup if you do get Brent to show for a signing," he commented.

"Tell me about it."

"No date set for the grand opening?"

"Not yet."

"I want a personal invite."

"You'll get one," she promised, sneaking a fry out of the bag. She thought that might be the end of the conversation, but Crash surprised her with some uncharacteristic diffidence.

"Listen, I, uh, wanted to ask you about your friend, Sue Ellen."

"What about her?"

"Think she would mind if I gave her a call?"

Mind? S.E. oozed hormones from every pore whenever she come within fifty feet of the studly major.

"Call away," she advised as she turned into the cul-de-sac leading to her rented home. "I'll give you a friendly warning, though. Sue Ellen's been burned twice. The last time was pretty bad."

"She told me a little about it the other night at your house."

Wedging the phone under her ear, Andi steered with one hand and hit the garage opener with the other. The door yawned up. Lights flooded the garage.

"Sue Ellen puts up a good front, Crash, but she's not as tough as she wants folks to think."

"I got that impression."

"Do you have her phone number?"

"I called information. She's unlisted."

"Chalk that up to creepo husband number two."

Andi knew Sue Ellen wouldn't mind if she shared the number with Crash. Hell, she might even pay a finder's fee. Grinning at the thought, Andi pulled into the garage and killed the engine.

"Just make sure you tell her how you got her number." She shouldered the door open and swung out. "I want—oooh!"

She'd moved too fast. The spots ballooned again, bigger and blacker than before.

"Andi?"

The concrete floor tilted under her feet. Her head spinning, she made a desperate grab for the Tahoe's door with her free hand.

"Andi, you okay?"

Crash's voice seemed to rise from the bottom of a deep, dark well. No, not a well. From the phone still clutched in her fist.

"Andi, talk to me!"

"Crash…"

She was sure she'd shouted his name, but all that came out was a hoarse croak. Worse, the effort caused another explosion of fuzzy dots. Needing both hands to cling to the door frame, Andi abandoned the phone.

It clattered to the concrete, bouncing a few times in the process. The back popped off on the first bounce. The battery spilled out on the second. The illuminated display went dead before the instrument finally settled.

Andi cursed but didn't dare release her death grip to bend over and scoop up the pieces until the haze cleared. Even then she went down slowly, hand over hand, inch by inch.

She'd probably scared the bejesus out of Crash. She had to call him back before he hit the panic button and dialed 911. Sinking to the concrete, she fumbled for her phone's guts.

She slid the battery in, snapped on the back and searched the directory for Crash's number. The numbers blurred, then cleared. Before she could press Call, however, footsteps pounded across the crushed-shell drive next door.

"Andi!"

The shout ricocheted through the night, deep and harsh and razored with something close to panic.

Oh, hell! Crash must have activated an emergency-response net that looped instantly from him to Sue Ellen to Dave.

Even as Andi braced herself for the storm she suspected would come, a treacherous relief rolled through her. She couldn't think of anyone she'd rather have charge to her rescue than Dave. Like most Special Ops types, he'd racked up enough medical training to qualify as an EMT.

Not that she needed an EMT. She was ninety-nine-point-nine percent certain the fuzzy spots sprang from her idiocy in forgetting to eat. It was the point-one percent that closed her throat and made her gulp with relief when her ex barreled into the garage.

Dave spotted Andi on the floor beside the Tahoe's open door and slowed his full-out sprint. His training went too deep to rush heedlessly to her side.

In two seconds flat he'd sized up the need for body substance isolation and assessed site safety. Reassured he wouldn't endanger Andi by setting a spark to spilled fuel or otherwise exacerbating a potentially lethal situation, he hunkered down beside her.

"What happened?"

Embarrassment and more than a touch of worry simmered in the depths of her green eyes, but they were clear and focused.

"I got a little dizzy while I was talking to Crash and, uh, dropped the phone."

Dave didn't touch her. Not yet. But he had to ball his fists as he searched for signs of trauma and his mind cataloged the critical ABCs. Airways open, with no apparent obstruction. Breathing rapid but even. Circulation okay, judging by her color.

"Do you still feel dizzy?"

"No. Just silly."

He found her pulse, strong and steady under the warm skin of her neck. "Any chest pains?"

"No."

"Nausea?"

"No."

"Damn!" Dave swallowed the foul taste of his fear and forced a grin. "And here I was hoping we'd have to go mouth-to-mouth."

That earned him a shaky laugh. Keeping his grin in place, he scooped her into his arms and carried her around the front end of the Tahoe.

"Let's get you to the ER."

"I'm okay now. Honestly. We don't need to hit the ER."

"Yeah, we do."

Biting her lip, Andi let him ease her into the passenger seat and click the seat belt into place. She sat silent while he called ahead and had Doc Ramirez paged. Despite her breezy assurances, those bouncing black spots had shaken her more than she wanted to admit.

Since Hurlburt Field operated only the day clinic, they had to drive the additional miles to the regional hospital at Eglin. Doc Ramirez was waiting at the ER. Her dark hair spilled over her shoulders, and her purple soccer shirt proudly proclaimed she was a Mustang Mom, but she brushed aside Andi's apologies for taking her away from her son's game.

"We were ahead three to one. My husband will cheer the team to victory. If you'll come with me, we'll check you over."

She flicked a glance at Dave, obviously weighing her patient's right to privacy against his very solid, very determined presence.

"Why don't you have a seat in the waiting room, Colonel? I'll let you know when we're done."

His jaw locked. A vein popped out on one temple. Hastily, Andi intervened.

"It's okay. I'd like him to come back with me."

"Your call," Ramirez said with a shrug. "This way, please."

THE ENTOURAGE SURROUNDING Andi soon included Dr. Ramirez, the attending ER physician, a nurse, a lab tech, an EKG specialist and Dave. Draped in a hospital gown, she was probed, poked and stuck.

The initial EKG results seemed to reassure the flight surgeons and eased some of the grim lines on Dave's face. After the EKG specialist wheeled away her cart and the lab tech trotted off with his blood samples, the docs withdrew to confer. Andi used the semiprivacy to peel off the disposable electrodes.

"You missed one," Dave commented.

She felt under the front opening of the hospital gown. "Where?"

"Here."

Chin tucked, he brushed her hand aside. His knuckles grazed her left breast en route to the stickie. As he tugged at the stubborn patch, Andi went very still. She could feel the adhesive stretching her skin, but that small sensation got lost in the others bombarding her.

His breath warmed her cheek. The familiar scent of him chased away the hospital smells. Heat from his skin transferred to hers. Or maybe it was the other way around. She still hadn't decided when a sharp rap sounded on the exam room door and Sue Ellen popped in.

Andi jerked, wincing as the stickie gave way with a section of her epidermis still attached. She looked up to find S.E.'s startled gaze fixed on the hand buried inside Andi's hospital gown.

"Sorry," her friend murmured, brows soaring. "They told me it was okay to come in."

"It is."

Unflustered, Dave withdrew his hand and deposited the electrode in the trash. Sue Ellen's brows went from full mast to straight-lined.

"What's the story? What happened, Andi?"

"I had a couple of dizzy spells. I'm pretty sure they sprang from the fact that I got so busy I forgot to eat." Flinging up a hand, she forestalled S.E.'s scathing comment. "That won't happen again."

"You think that's all it was? Really?"

"Really. So does my cardiologist. The EKG was normal and my heart sounded strong. If the blood work comes back okay, they're going to send me home."

S.E. speared a glance in Dave's direction.

"Don't worry," he drawled. "I'll feed her before I tuck her in for the night."

Sue Ellen looked as though she wanted to comment on the tucking-in part. Particularly after the scene she'd walked in on a few moments ago. Thankfully she refrained. Andi wasn't sure she could explain those breathless moments to anyone's satisfaction, her own included.

Just when she thought she'd skated, her friend jumped on another sensitive topic.

"I don't understand. You were having dizzy spells and you called Crash? Why didn't you call me? I'm closer. Or Dave, for God's sake."

With her back to Dave, S.E. didn't notice his sudden frown but Andi bore the full brunt of it. Her ex's expression reminded her forcibly of the awkward moment in her kitchen, when he'd discovered her in the younger man's arms.

"I wondered that myself," Dave bit out.

"I didn't call Crash. He called me. To get Sue Ellen's phone number," Andi tacked on as Dave's expression hardened.

"Really?"

Sue Ellen didn't go so far as to purr, but her smile conveyed a distinctly feline satisfaction.

"I'd better call him back and let him know how you're doing. The poor baby was soooo worried about you."

CHAPTER 9

Jim's Café dished up the best hamburgers and home fries in northwest Florida and was a favorite hangout for Special Tactics troops. Dave acknowledged the greeting of several men in jeans and variations of camouflage gear as he steered Andi to a booth tucked back in a corner. Stale cigarette smoke drifted in from the bar but couldn't compete with the ambrosia of sizzling onions and charbroiled meat.

Dave didn't bother with a menu. "Two Number Fours," he instructed the waitress. "Load 'em up with fried onions, go light on the mayo and hold the pickles." He hooked a brow in Andi's direction. "Right?"

"Right."

Four years, and he remembered her aversion to anything and everything cucumberish. The knowledge warmed the small part of her not focused on the monster platters being delivered to the couple in the next booth. Those heaping plates reminded Andi of how hungry she was…and how dumb it was to go all day without eating.

"Sorry you have to keep charging to my rescue," she

said, embarrassed all over again at her stupidity. "Last week the bookshelves, tonight a trip to the ER."

"I like charging to your rescue. It makes for a nice change."

"What do you mean?"

"You never needed me before."

"That's not true!"

Dave had tossed the comment out without thinking. Her startled response made him reconsider its impact.

"Yeah, babe," he said slowly, "it is. Looking back, I think neither one of us really needed the other."

Surprise and hurt darkened her eyes. "How can you say that? We were consumed with need. I wanted you from the first night we met. I know, those first years, you wanted me every bit as much."

"You're right. I did. Still do."

She went stiff. "Dave..."

"Don't worry. I promised I wouldn't push you and I won't."

The rigidity went out of her shoulders, but the hurt lingered in her eyes. "What are you saying then? That wanting each other doesn't equate to love?"

"I *think* I'm saying want is only a part of love. There should be respect..."

"There was," she countered. "We've always respected each other's drive and dedication."

"And commitment…"

"Okay, we screwed up that part. We let our commitment to our jobs get in the way of our marriage."

"And need," Dave finished. "There should be more than physical craving."

"I needed you, dammit."

"For what?"

"For a thousand things!" She flapped an impatient hand. "Balancing the checkbook. Setting the timers on the sprinkler system. Picking up our uniforms at the laundry when I couldn't get there."

"Real heavy stuff…and nothing you didn't do yourself when I wasn't around."

"I'm not sure I understand where you're coming from with this," she said stiffly. "What did you want from me? Weak and helpless?"

"Could you have done either?"

"No." Angry now, she slapped her shoulder blades against the back of the booth. "Neither could you, if I might point out the obvious."

"True."

"Let's turn this around," she said, still ruffled. "What did you need me for?"

Dave shagged a hand through his hair. He'd started this. He had to finish.

"If you want the truth, I didn't know how much I

needed you until after we split. The longer we were apart, the more I missed scraping you off the ceiling when headquarters issued what you considered another idiotic directive. I missed the way you always insist on ordering pepperoni on your pizza and proceed to pick it all off. I even missed your nasty habit of using my razor to shave your legs, then forgetting to tell me the blade was dull."

"Real heavy stuff," she mocked, echoing his previous refrain.

Dave figured he'd waded in this far, he might as well go for the deep water.

"The truth is, losing you left a gaping hole in my life. I've learned to live with it, but it sure makes for empty days and long nights."

He waited for her reaction, smiling a little to mask the intensity of his feelings.

He'd run the full gamut tonight, from the stark terror that had sent him sprinting across the drive to Andi's house to crushing relief to teeth-grinding irritation that she'd brought tonight's crisis on herself. He'd refrained from chewing her up one side and down the other for that bit of stupidity. Barely. Now here he was spilling his guts, while she frowned and fiddled with the saltshaker.

"How sad," she said after a moment. "And how ironic considering it was the endless succession of long days and empty nights that convinced us to call it quits."

"Convinced *you* to call it quits," he reminded her quietly. "I wanted to hang in there."

"I know." Sighing, she aligned the salt beside the pepper. "I guess you put your finger on the underlying problem. We never really blended our lives. We were both too independent, too self-sufficient." She lifted her gaze to his. "That hasn't changed."

"Doesn't mean it can't. Just something to think about," he added as the waitress approached with two steaming platters.

DAVE HAD FORGOTTEN ABOUT the impetus behind Andi's call to his office earlier that afternoon. He didn't remember the camera until he'd seen her into her house and retreated to his own. The camcorder sat on the hall table where he'd left it, waiting patiently. Retracing his steps, he delivered it to her front door.

"We forgot this in all the excitement."

"So we did."

"You'll need to charge the battery. I haven't used it in a while."

More than a while. He hadn't had the thing out of its box since the Christmas she'd given it to him. They'd split soon afterward, and Dave hadn't felt the urge to record home movies in the years since. A digital still camera more than suited his needs.

Burying the painful memories, he waited while she unzipped the case and extracted the camera.

"Got a minute to show me how it works?"

"Sure."

He followed her into the high-ceilinged great room. As he had the night he'd joined her and her guests for dinner, he searched the room for mementos from their shared past. She'd rented the place furnished, he knew, and put most of her household goods in storage. But he recognized the framed watercolor of Bangkok's floating market. They'd bought it on the first of three days and two steamy nights they'd spent in that fascinating city.

He also recognized several of the critters in her crystal menagerie. He'd brought the penguin with him as a homecoming gift after a session of highly specialized Arctic training. The unicorn he'd picked up during a layover in Ireland. The blowfish, he remembered with slicing regret, had joined the ranks after a deployment had forced him to cancel a long-scheduled vacation in Hawaii.

Andi had worn the same uniform, was subject to the same short-notice deployments and disruptions of personal plans. She'd groused a bit but hadn't whined or complained about the cancellation.

Would things have turned out differently if she had? If either of them had put the other's needs before those of their troops or their service or their country? If they hadn't been so damned independent and self-sufficient?

His glance shifted to Andi, hunkered down on the sofa with the camera and its peripherals spread out before her on the coffee table. She'd claimed at the café that nothing had changed. His response came back to haunt him.

Doesn't mean it can't.

She looked up then, a black bud pinched between her fingers. "This is the remote mike, right?"

"Right."

"How do you activate it?"

"Beats me."

He joined her on the sofa. Knee to knee, they went through the instruction manual.

"Why do you need the remote?" he asked, frowning at the complicated diagrams. "The built-in mike picks up all sounds within a reasonable range."

"I might have to place the camera some distance from my subject."

"Are you taking shots of the store?"

"Some shots *in* the store. The building inspector who's holding up my occupancy permit is doing another walk-through tomorrow." Flicking to the next page, she skimmed the instructions. "Wayne Jacobs, my leasing agent, says the guy won't approve the permit until we slip him some cash. I'm hoping he tries to put the squeeze on me tomorrow."

"Whoa! You want this camcorder to record a crooked inspector soliciting or accepting a bribe?"

"That's the plan."

"You can't do that, Andi."

"Sure I can."

"No, you can't!"

He yanked the instruction book out of her hands to get her attention.

"There are laws against secretly recording or disclosing private conversations."

"Give me some credit, Armstrong. I went online and checked the statutes. Under Florida law, you don't need consent to record an oral communication uttered by someone who doesn't have a reasonable expectation of privacy."

"I doubt your inspector expects his oral communications to be made public."

"He may not, but if more than two people are present during the discussion, he's screwed." Smug satisfaction laced her reply. "Technically a three-party conversation is no longer private."

Dave struggled heroically to hang on to his temper. They'd just made a trip to the ER, for God's sake. She should be taking it easy, recouping her strength after those dizzy spells. Instead she was plotting the downfall of a crooked building inspector.

"Who's your third party?"

"Wayne Jacobs, my leasing agent. He and I are meeting the inspector at two tomorrow, in my shop. Although…"

Frowning, she clicked her nails against the camcorder's case.

"So far Wayne's refused to cough up a cent. The target might get suspicious if he does an abrupt about-face."

Target. Christ!

Dave was marshaling all the reasons she shouldn't set herself up as the next James Bond when she slanted him a speculative glance.

"What are you doing around two tomorrow afternoon, Armstrong?"

"Get real, Andi. You think this guy will talk with a stranger present?"

"Not a stranger. My business partner. Or we could go with the truth and say you're my ex-husband. You've invested a bundle," she improvised, "staked me to part of the start-up costs because you still feel guilty about walking out on me. Now you just want to get me off your back."

"Weak. Very weak."

"Hey, it can work."

Springing off the sofa, she threw herself into the role of abandoned wife.

"You've been paying alimony, but it stops when—if— I begin earning income from the shop. You want that to happen. You *need* it to happen, since the twin stepkids you inherited when you remarried just entered college."

"Care to tell me which college?"

Magnanimously, she left the choice to him. "You pick the school. Make it private and out of state, though. The tuition costs are busting your balls."

Something certainly was, and that something stood just a few feet away, her entire body alive with the vibrant energy she brought to every task, big or small. Dave gave up all thought of trying to rein her in.

"Just out of curiosity," he drawled, "how does my current wife feel about having you for a neighbor?"

"She's pissed. Really pissed. But you've got orders, so you'll depart the area in a few months. Before you leave, you want to make sure I get the shop up and running."

"You missed your calling, woman. You should have specialized in undercover ops."

"It's never too late to develop new skills." After a few more embellishments, his coconspirator shoved her hands in the pockets of her jeans. "Think you can remember all that?"

"Ex-wife. Alimony. Twins. Private university. Got it."

Pushing to his feet, Dave made for the door. "This is just lame enough to work. See you at fourteen hundred tomorrow, Armstrong."

"Not if I see you first."

HER MIND SPINNING WITH the details of her plot, Andi went back to the camcorder. As Dave had warned, the battery was stone-cold dead.

She plugged the charger into a wall outlet and connected the other end to the camera. The instrument beeped to life in her hands.

"Okay, sweetheart, let's see what you can do."

Following the instructions, she opened the viewing screen and switched from still to movie mode. Activating the remote mike required additional references to the manual.

Now to see if it worked.

Aiming the telescopic lens at the far corner of the great room, Andi slipped the supersensitive mike into her shirt pocket and crossed to the far corner of the room.

"Testing, one, two, three."

For good measure, she opened the sliding glass doors to add a chorus of night sounds to her test. Cicadas chirped, the bug lights popped as an unwary mosquito got zapped and the sea murmured restlessly in the distance.

"Testing, one, two, three."

When she went to review the test, the sound played back with astonishing clarity, but the video screen remained blank.

Hell! She must have hit the wrong setting. Not hard to do, since the minicam came packed with enough variations to record a full-length animated feature film. Wondering how engineers managed to cram so many options into such a small case, Andi reread the manual and tried again. This time the tiny viewing screen lit up.

"Yes!"

She hit the reverse button, saw a blur of colorful scenes whir by and had to search for the stop button. She was about to fast-forward again when the three-inch screen filled with bright, colorful lights.

"What's this?"

A Christmas tree, she saw as the camera zoomed out, its lights twinkling against stressed-oak paneling. With a jolt, she recognized the paneling. She'd picked it for the den of the last home she and Dave had shared.

Have you figured it out yet?

Her disembodied voice floated through the camcorder's speaker. Dave's deep baritone followed.

I think so.

The camera panned, jerked to a stop and zoomed in

on a creature sitting cross-legged amid a pile of un-
wrapped presents, her hair in wild tangles and a Santa
Claus coffee mug poised halfway to her lips.

Smile, Andi. Better yet, wave and sing "Jingle Bells."

Uh-uh! You know I can't carry a tune in a duffel bag.

Be a sport, Mrs. Claus. Croon for the camera.

No.

The woman in the video made a face and hid behind
her Santa mug. The woman watching her blinked away
the prick of hot, stinging tears.

*Jeez, you're stubborn. Guess I'll have to mount this on
the tripod and get in the shot with you. We'll make it a duet.*

Walls and floor tilted as the camera swung crazily. A
thump sounded. The view leveled. Dave had plunked his
Christmas present on the coffee table, Andi remembered, her throat tight and aching.

As he rustled through boxes and wadded paper for the
tripod she'd bought to go with the camera, the camcorder's sensitive mike magnified the sounds. Every crack
and crackle seemed to stab into Andi's chest.

How do you hook up this thing?

How do I know?

There was a rattle, a whoosh of pneumatic legs telescop-
ing, then floor and ceiling upended again. Finally Dave
connected camcorder and stand. Seconds later he waded
into Andi's nest of wrapping paper and dropped beside her.

Dashing through the snow…

Belting out the old standard at the top of his lungs, Dave tried to get her to join him.

In a one-horse open sleigh…

Oh, God!

Cradling the camera in both hands, Andi slid off the sofa cushion onto the floor. Her agonized gaze stayed locked on the small screen. She knew what would come next.

Dave mugging for the camera.

Finishing his solo with a hearty ho-ho-ho.

Tugging her onto his lap for a kiss.

Plucking the mug out of her hand and setting it aside before he tumbled her into the mounds of paper.

He'd tried hard to patch things up that Christmas. So had she. Their last desperate attempt to make their marriage work had only delayed the inevitable.

"Dammit!"

Her palm hit the screen, snapping it shut. The camcorder bounced to the carpet. She couldn't watch any more.

She'd put the past behind her. Or thought she had. Now Dave was back in her life and determined to try again. Could she let him in? Did she have the will to keep him out?

She knew the answer before she retrieved the camera. They'd tried long-distance marriage once. It didn't work then. It wouldn't work now...unless they took a lesson from past mistakes and figured out how to blend.

Pushing to her feet, she zipped the camcorder into its case.

CHAPTER 10

"Morning, sir."

Captain Acker snapped to attention. Returning his greeting, Dave snagged a mug of coffee and made a beeline for his office.

"What's on the agenda today?"

Acker followed, toting the morning file. "Stand-up at seven. Briefing on the accident board's preliminary report at eight. Colonel Johnson's on for ten-twenty to go over CINCSOUTH's request for an additional combat controller team for Operation Southern Watch. This afternoon you wanted to observe the Navy's new protocol for underwater egress training at Pensacola. I've scheduled a staff car to pick you up at thirteen hundred."

"Cancel the staff car and reschedule the visit. I have some personal business to I need to take care of this afternoon.'"

Like playing an exasperated ex-husband.

Dave wouldn't have to dig very deep for the role. He

still hadn't quite recovered from last night's trip to the ER, precipitated by Andi's idiocy in forgetting to eat.

"What about the major's selection board, sir? The colonel's group needs to know if you'll take it or if we're sending Colonel Heath instead. We promised them a reply no later than this afternoon."

Dave gulped down a swig of coffee. Sitting on a promotion board was both an honor and an obligation. Dave and his fellow board members would review thousands of sharp young captains and select only the best and the brightest for promotion to major. More to the point, Dave would be representing the Special Ops community. He owed it to the promotion-eligible officers in his command to share his knowledge of their unique skills with the other colonels on the board.

Yet the board would run for a minimum of three weeks. Hard on its heels was a swing through the Pacific, where Dave was supposed to tour Combat Rescue units assigned to bases in the Far East with the new PACAF commander.

That was five weeks minimum away from his office. Away from Andi.

He took another swig of coffee and skimmed the stark black-and-white photos mounted on the wall. Those were his troops in the pictures, his responsibility.

Other images kept superimposing themselves over the

photos. Andi on the floor of her garage. Andi with a green hospital gown slipping down one shoulder. Andi peeling off sticky-backed electrodes.

"Tell the colonel's group we're sending Colonel Heath."

DAVE PARKED HIS PICKUP outside Andi's shop at one-forty.

She'd been on the lookout for him. Glancing up from the camera she was concealing behind some boxes on one of the bookshelves, she noted with approval that he'd changed out of his uniform.

Good thinking. In boots, BDUs and beret, with his eagles bristling on his collar, he came across as authoritative and more than a little intimidating. Since their script called for exasperation and impatience rather than intimidation, it would play better in civvies.

Not that Dave Armstrong looked all that much *less* threatening in cords, a Hawaiian shirt and an Atlanta Braves ball cap. With his square, uncompromising jaw and don't-mess-with-me stride, the man was a walking billboard for macho.

Once inside the shop, he paused by the refinished counter and searched the rows of bookshelves. "Andi?"

"Right here."

Angling the lens to make sure she had him squarely in the viewfinder, she switched the camera to Off to save the battery and joined him at the front of the store. His gaze skimmed her snug jeans and gauzy leopard-print top before locking on her face.

"Any more dizzy spells?"

"None."

"What have you eaten today?"

"Breakfast, lunch *and* a PowerBar."

With a small grunt, he splayed his hands on his hips. Andi assumed the inarticulate sound signified approval of her improved dietary habits and launched into her prebrief.

"The inspector's name is Kevin Talbot. Wayne Jacobs, my leasing agent, says he goes by Bud. Reportedly Buddy boy retired from the…the…"

She stumbled to a halt, her startled glance drawn to the gold band on his left hand. The brushed gold stood out like neon against his tanned skin. Its unique basket-weave pattern was achingly familiar.

"You're…" Dragging in a quick breath, she fought the tide of memories threatening to swamp her. "You're wearing your wedding ring."

He flexed his hand and glanced down at the ring. "I'm supposed to be married. Thought I'd better dress the part." He looked up, snagging her in a hard vise. "Do you still have yours?"

"It's, uh, in the box that holds my ribbons and rank insignia."

None of which she wore any longer. Feeling suddenly adrift and cut off from the lifelines that had anchored her for so many years, Andi swiped her tongue over her lips and picked up where she'd left off.

"Our boy Bud retired from the construction business up in Michigan five or six years ago and moved to Florida. Since Gulf Springs is too small for a full-time building inspector, Talbot fills in part-time at the request of the mayor and town council."

"Supplementing his retirement income with a bribe or two."

"That's our working theory. I've reconfirmed the two o'clock appointment. Wayne was going to arrive then, too, but I told him to come late. I want Buddy boy to walk in on you and me slinging barbs at each other about alimony, tuition costs and the delays in getting the shop open."

"Right. The twins are attending Duke, by the way."

"Duke. Got it."

"Jenny's pulling straight A's. Jake fell for a cute little freshman and is barely scraping through this semester. Trish is really torqued about that. The current Mrs. Armstrong," he added at Andi's blank look. "She's a redhead, in case you're interested."

"I'm not. Here's the plan. We'll let Talbot check the new sprinkler heads and see what he comes up with. If he signs off on the occupancy permit, we're home free.

If he doesn't, we need to position him by the counter, about where you're standing now. I've got the camera set for wide-angle to get us all in. The mike's pinned right here, under my blouse."

She patted the spangles banding the neckline of the splashy print blouse. Additional sparkles highlighted the busy leopard pattern. Buddy boy would have to put his nose smack-dab in the middle of her chest to notice the mike amid all those gaudy, glittery spots.

To her consternation, Dave did almost that. Hooking a finger in the V-neck of her blouse, he tugged her across the counter for a closer inspection of the hidden device.

"Show me."

"It's right here."

Andi tugged the spangled neck band aside, wishing she hadn't worn a push-up bra, perversely happy she had. The heat that sprang into Dave's eyes as he searched for the mike warmed her all the way down to her toes.

His voice was low and gruff when he released her. "How do you figure to segue from sprinkler heads to under-the-counter payoffs?"

"That's your job. I would suggest you go all huffy and act like the delays are my fault. Then you might pull Talbot aside and ask him man to man what it would take to get me off your back."

"That sounds pretty close to entrapment."

"I checked the statutes on that, too. A person is only 'entrapped' when he's persuaded by law enforcement officers or their agents to commit a crime he had no intention of committing. A, we're not law enforcement officers, just ordinary citizens. B, if we catch this guy on camera soliciting a bribe, it probably won't stand up as evidence in a court of law, but it *should* get the attention of the mayor and/or the town council."

"You want to tread carefully here, Andi. This guy isn't going to take kindly to being exposed."

"I pulled two tours at the Pentagon," she reminded him tartly, "and one in Iraq. I can handle whatever Buddy boy throws my way."

THE SCRIPT COULDN'T have played any better if it had been penned by a team of ace Hollywood screenwriters.

Andi stayed on the watch for Talbot and darted back to activate the camera when his panel truck pulled into a parking space outside the shop. She reverified the angle, checked to make sure the correct date and time showed in the viewfinder and squared her shoulders.

Showtime, folks.

When Talbot was a half step from the front door, she launched herself into her role and stalked to the front of the shop.

"Dammit, Armstrong! I *told* you these delays aren't my fault."

On cue, Dave plunged into his frustrated-ex act. "Yeah, right. I know you, woman. I should, after living with you for all those excruciating years. You construct detailed checklists for everything from brushing your teeth to prepositioning combat troops in a war zone."

That hit a little too close to home. Bristling, Andi made sure they were both facing away from the door and followed his lead.

"So?" She didn't have to dig too deep for the belligerence that colored her reply.

"So you would have planned for any unexpected contingencies and found a work-around by now. Admit it, Andi. You're dragging your feet so you can bank those friggin' alimony checks every month."

"You walk," she drawled, "you pay. And you'll continue to pay until I get this shop up and running."

They were nose-to-nose now, giving their best imitation of twin volcanoes about to erupt. Steam vented from every fissure. Andi could almost smell the sulfur.

"Tell your skinny-assed new wife to stop whining," she jeered. "I'll let you off the hook. It's just taking a little longer than I anticipated."

Behind them, Talbot cleared his throat. They both ignored him.

"Trish doesn't whine," Dave fired back. "Although God knows you've given her plenty of reason to with all your—"

"'Scuse me, folks."

Snarling, Dave rounded on the building inspector. "Who the hell are you?"

Buddy boy blinked and took a quick step back. He was a tall, spare man with pens poking from the pocket of his blue plaid shirt. A clipboard was tucked under one arm.

"My name's Bud Talbot. I'm supposed to meet Wayne Jacobs here to check the new sprinkler heads."

"Wayne's been delayed," Andi replied, projecting the image of a woman heroically trying to rein in her temper. "I'm Andrea Armstrong. This is my shop. Or will be when you and the town council approve my permit. Which," she tacked on with another sneer in Dave's direction, "certain people seem to think I'm deliberately dragging my feet on."

Talbot cleared his throat again. "Maybe I can expedite matters. Let me take a look at the sprinkler heads."

Andi left Dave drumming his fingers on the counter and accompanied the inspector on his walk-through. The new sprinklers showed bright and shiny against the freshly painted ceiling. Talbot annotated the make, model and number of each on his clipboard.

"Looks like you're up to code," he announced, pocketing his pen.

Andi didn't have to fake her sigh of relief. She wouldn't hesitate to take down a crooked inspector but much preferred dealing with an honest one.

"Make sure you keep at least eighteen inches of clearance between the heads and the tops of those shelves," Talbot advised.

"I will."

"Good. Now all you have to do is show me your certificate and I'll be out of your hair."

"What certificate?"

"For the sprinkler system. Regulations require that you post the manufacturer's certificate next to a schedule of inspections. You need to include the name of the person authorized to conduct the inspection on the schedule."

"Wayne must have the certificate. I'll retrieve it from him and hang it today. I'll also make up the required schedule."

When the pen emerged from Talbot's pocket once again, Andi realized she'd sighed too soon.

"Sorry, ma'am. I can't recommend approval of your permit until I see both the certificate and the schedule. We'll have to arrange another walk-though."

"You're kidding!"

"I don't kid about building safety."

"I'll get the certificate from Wayne, I promise. And if

you'll tell me how often I need to conduct these inspections, I'll draft a schedule right now."

Talbot shook his head. "I hate to be such a stickler, ma'am, but rules are rules. Jacobs should have taken care of all this for you," he grumbled, neatly passing the blame. "I'll come back when he has."

Andi threw Dave what she very much hoped was a weak and helpless look. She must have pulled off at least one of the two, as Talbot didn't appear surprised when her ex stepped in and took charge.

"Call Jacobs," he instructed Andi tersely. "Ask him if he's got the damned certificate. Bud, what do you say we talk about this man to man?"

Andi retreated to the back of the shop and made a show of digging her cell phone out of her purse. All the while she kept the mike embedded in her neckline pointed toward the men at the counter. They were well within recording range, but she sweated bullets as they put their heads together.

Dave spoke first, fast and low. Talbot listened, glancing Andi's way and nodding a few times before answering. She pretended not to see him or notice when Dave seemed to hesitate for several moments.

And when he reached into his back pocket and extracted his wallet, she had to restrain herself from punching a fist into the air.

Yes!

She considered confronting Talbot then and there but needed to be sure she'd captured him on tape. Otherwise he could deny everything and it would just be their word against his.

While the inspector palmed the bill Dave passed him, Andi confirmed with Wayne Jacobs that he was indeed in possession of the manufacturer's certificate. She also confirmed that inspections were required monthly.

"Thanks, Wayne."

"Talbot still there?"

"He is."

"How's it going?"

"Excellently. Talk to you later."

Snapping the phone shut, she grabbed her notebook and tore out a lined page. Two bold slashes divided the sheet into columns. She labeled the first *Date*, the second *Name of Inspector* and the third *Status*. A few quick scribbles filled in the entry for September.

"Here's my inspection schedule. Wayne has the certificate in his car. He'll deliver it in person within the hour."

Talbot rubbed the side of his nose. "I've got another appointment I have to go to. Guess I could swing back by here afterward. Say four-thirty? That way I can verify that I saw the appropriate documents."

Feigning both gratitude and delight, Andi beamed

him a smile. "Thanks, Bud. I certainly wouldn't want you to break the rules."

With a shrug and a nod to Dave, Buddy boy went on his larcenous way. Andi waited until he'd backed his panel truck out of the parking space and driven off before whirling to face her coconspirator.

"Did what I think happened really happen?"

"It did."

Dave didn't go in for displays of emotion, but she could tell from the wicked satisfaction lacing his voice that he was as pumped as she was.

"You owe me two hundred bucks, woman."

"If that camera works as advertised, I'll pay you back shortly…with interest!"

"I can wait for the two hundred." With a slashing grin, he burrowed a hand under her hair. "How about I take the interest in advance?"

Gulping, Andi did her best to ignore the sudden heat searing her nape. "You promised, Armstrong. No pushing."

"I'm not pushing, babe. I'm pulling."

The tug was so slight, the movement so slow, his muscles barely flexed. All Andi needed to do to break his hold was pull back an inch or two.

She meant to. She really did. She had too much coming down on her right now to give in to the insane need to feel his mouth on hers again.

But Armstrong had always known which buttons to press and when to press them. The thrill of getting Buddy boy on tape still bubbled through her veins, and the stroke of Dave's thumb along the sensitive spot just below her ear only heightened the thrill. In mere seconds Andi went from excited and triumphant to just plain excited.

And alive! God, so very alive.

Riding a rush of exuberance and unleashed lust, she threw herself into the kiss. Her mouth locked with his. Her tongue got busy. Every inch of her leaped to life as she slicked her hands over his shoulders and locked them around his neck.

Dave's reaction was swift and erotic. Widening his stance, he canted her hips into his. All it took was one contact for Andi to feel him, stiff as a telephone pole, against her belly. Her womb clenched in an ancient and totally primal response.

She wanted this man, wanted to drag him down behind the counter and yield to the rutting instincts imprinted in the DNA of every species on Earth.

Dave was her mate. He wore her brand, the gold band that had marked him as hers. Once.

Then her mind shut down and her body took charge. She pressed closer, grinding her mouth into his, flattening her chest against his—and got stabbed in the breast.

"Ow!"

She jumped back, breaking Dave's hold. His head jerked up. Fear washed the heat from his cheeks.

"What?"

"The mike." Wincing, she reached inside the neckline of her blouse. "The damned thing gouged a hole in me."

His breath left on a loud rattle. Muttering a curse, he slumped against the counter and waited while she extracted the microphone. She was twirling the tiny bud between her fingers when she remembered the camcorder aimed in their direction.

"Oh, hell! I left the camera on. The battery's probably run down."

"Mine hasn't."

Dave reached for her again, but they both knew the wild, reckless moment had passed. Digging deep for a smile, Andi shook her head.

"It's good we stopped when we did."

"You think so, huh?"

She knew so. The Christmas video had ripped a hole in her heart. She could imagine the damage an X-rated version would do.

"This is happening too fast, Dave. I told you—I need time to think."

"Yeah, you did." He brushed a knuckle down her

cheek. "But I have to say I like it better when we don't think and just go with our instincts."

"That's what we did the first time around. This time—if there's going to *be* a this time—we need to do it right. You said as much last night. We have to learn how to weave our separate lives into a single whole."

He skimmed a glance around the shop, brought it back to her.

"This place is a start, Andi. I know I muscled my way in, but I like watching you bring it to life. And I had fun this afternoon…during *and* after Talbot's visit. Thanks for including me in your scam."

"Speaking of which, I'd better check the camera and see if we caught Bud on tape."

Andi retrieved the camcorder and saw the batteries hadn't completely run down. Setting the device on the counter, she flipped out the viewing screen and hit rewind.

The display showed a blur of backward motion. Turkey gobbles of distorted sound filled the air. Leaning over her shoulder, Dave squinted at the tiny screen.

"There! Stop!"

The image sharpened to incredible clarity. Better yet, the turkey gobbles dissolved into distinctly audible dialogue.

…do you say we talk about this man to man?

There was Talbot, his glance shifting between Dave and Andi.

What do we have to talk about?

As I think you heard, my alimony payments are killing me. I'm hoping to get out from under them—and get my ex-wife off my ass once her shop is open for business. How do I make that happen?

Man to man?

Man to man.

Two hundred should do it.

"Hot damn!" Whooping, Andi hit the freeze-frame button. "You did it, Armstrong. You got Talbot to hang himself out to dry."

He wasn't quite as elated as she was. "What are you going to do with the tape?"

"Show it to Buddy boy when he comes back at four-thirty and retrieve your two hundred, for starters. Then I'll take it to the mayor. I doubt if the town council will hire Talbot to conduct future inspections."

She unfroze the video and watched the rest of the small drama. Satisfaction and real gratitude colored her voice when she turned to Dave.

"Thanks for helping with this."

"You're welcome."

"Want to stick around a while and catch act two?"

"I'd planned to."

"Why?" She cocked her head, sensing there was more behind his comment than mere curiosity as to how the final act in the drama would spin out. "Do you think Talbot might turn mean?"

"You corner a junkyard dog, he'll go for your throat. Never hurts to have some backup, babe."

CHAPTER 11

By the time Bud Talbot returned, Andi had mounted the sprinkler system manufacturer's certificate alongside a more professional-looking inspection schedule. She'd also rewound the camcorder to the appropriate spot and had it waiting on the counter.

Dave sprawled in one of the shop's overstuffed easy chairs. Wayne Jacobs occupied the other. Still jazzed from a sneak preview of the tape, the agent had begged Andi to let him stick around for the official showing.

Backed by so much testosterone, she was ready when the inspector reentered her shop. He looked surprised to see Dave still hanging around after the acrimonious exchange he'd overheard earlier and dipped his head to acknowledge Wayne.

"You bring that certificate, Jacobs?"

"Sure did. Ms. Armstrong has it posted at the back of the store, along with her inspection schedule."

"I'll just take a gander and be on my way."

Andi accompanied him to the rear of the shop and indicated the framed certificate with a little flourish.

Talbot leaned in, squinting at the date. The pen came out of his pocket. Two ticks on his clipboard later, he handed her a copy of his final walk-through inspection recommending approval of her occupancy permit.

"Looks good, Ms. Armstrong. Far as I'm concerned, you're ready to open for business."

"Almost." Tucking the form into the pocket of her jeans, Andi led the way back toward the front of the shop. "There's another small matter I need to discuss with you first."

"What's that?"

"The two-hundred-dollar bribe my ex-husband paid you."

Talbot stopped in his tracks and zinged a glance at the two men ensconced in the easy chairs.

"He said he gave me two hundred dollars?"

"He did. Do you deny it?"

"Maybe I do and maybe I don't. Seems like that would be a matter between me and him."

"This is my shop, Mr. Talbot. I'm responsible for whatever happens on these premises."

"You'd better tell that to your ex—"

"You're right." Folding her arms, Andi sang out, "Dave! Mr. Talbot says to remind you this is my shop."

"So?"

"So I don't want you bribing him or anyone else on my behalf."

"Hell," Talbot muttered. "That wasn't a bribe!"

"Really? What would you call it?"

"It was, uh, a commission."

Andi didn't bother to hide her disdain. "A commission for what?"

"Your ex-husband asked for my professional advice."

He turned to Dave, obviously expecting him to back up the story and extricate them both from this jam. All he received was cool silence from Dave and a snort of derision from Wayne Jacobs.

"She's nailed you, Talbot."

"The hell she has."

Whirling back to Andi, the inspector tried to bluff his way out. "Look, your ex wanted my advice on what he could do to get the shop open and you off his ass. Those were his exact words. I'm telling you, he practically reached over and stuffed the money in my shirt pocket."

"Funny, it plays differently on the video."

"Video?" Talbot's face turned gray under his Florida tan. "What video?"

"The one I shot while you two were having your man-to-man chat. I left the tape in the camera," she said, directing his attention to the camcorder with a sweep of one hand. "I thought you might like to watch the replay before I show it to the mayor."

The inspector's eyes cut to Andi's face. The combination of anger and desperation she saw in them reminded her all too forcefully of Dave's warning about junkyard dogs.

"All right," he ground out. "Guess we can both play this game. How much do you want for that tape?"

"It's not for sale."

"Sure it is," he countered roughly. "The first rule in business is to turn a profit whenever you can. Here's your chance. How much?"

Dave came out of his chair. "You heard the lady, Talbot. The tape isn't for sale."

Wayne rose, as well, a look of intense satisfaction on his face. Andi suspected he'd put up with too much crap from the inspector over the years to be left out of the fun.

"You put the squeeze on the wrong folks this time, Talbot. Now I suggest you return your two-hundred-dollar *commission* and start looking for another part-time job. After Ms. Armstrong and I talk to the mayor, you won't be conducting any more building inspections in Gulf Springs. And don't try to play any more games with her business permit. We all heard you say the shop met specs."

Red rushed into Talbot's cheeks. Without another

word, he dragged the folded bills out of his pocket. His face was ugly when he slapped them on the counter and slammed out the front door.

"I think we just put a serious dent in the man's day," Andi commented as his truck tore away from the curb.

"Day, week and month," Wayne agreed.

Dave didn't appear as elated as they were at the outcome. Frowning, he followed Talbot's truck until it disappeared around a corner.

"You've made an enemy there, Andi. You'd better check six for a while."

"I always watch my back," she returned, already leaping ahead to the next steps in her master plan.

Books! Now she could order her initial stock of books. And call the sign maker to confirm delivery. And contact the part-timer who wanted to work for her. And fix a date for her store opening. And e-mail Roger Brent.

Oh, God! If she could nail the thriller author for the grand opening…

Almost dancing with impatience, she grabbed her purse.

"I'm off to see Bernice. Then I'll deliver the video to the mayor. Want to drive over with me, Wayne?"

"You bet."

Her mind buzzing, Andi stuffed the camcorder in her bag and treated Dave to a hundred-watt smile. "Thanks for playing the heavy for me, Armstrong."

"Anytime, Armstrong."

"I owe you one."

"Yeah, you do."

"You'll have to tell me how I can square things between us."

His mouth curved. "I'll give it serious consideration."

WHEN ANDI WAVED HER copy of the approved final inspection at Bernice, the beaming town clerk waddled to her computer and printed out the business permit on the spot.

When she played the video in the office of the used-car dealership owned by the man currently serving as Gulf Springs's mayor, Al Frost's reaction was more tempered.

"I've heard rumors about Talbot," he admitted, scratching his chin. "Never could get anyone to step forward and separate rumor from fact."

"I'd say the video does just that," Andi replied, "in digital sound and color."

"It's pretty damning, all right. I'm just not sure it's enough to prosecute. I'll have to consult with the attorney we keep on retainer and lay the matter before the other members of the town council."

"I've accomplished my goals. I'll leave the rest to you and the council."

"Speaking of which…"

Frost tipped back in his chair. Unlike most of his constituents, he'd somehow managed to avoid acquiring any trace of a tan. As a result, the liver spots dotting his pale skin stood out like swatted flies.

"One of our council members up and quit last month. I've been looking for someone to fill his unexpired term. You interested?"

"Good Lord, no!"

Frost didn't appear to take offense at the somewhat less than polite response. Smiling, he enlisted the man seated beside Andi in his cause.

"Jacobs here has been singing your praises ever since you decided to open shop in Gulf Springs. From what I hear, you possess just the kind of top-level management and financial savvy we need on the council."

She gave the leasing agent a dry look. "Thanks a lot, friend."

Unrepentant, Wayne jumped on the bandwagon. "Al's right. You'd be a terrific addition to the council."

"Not while I'm trying to get my business up and running."

"Most all the councilmen operate some sort of enterprise," Frost put in. "You could network with other business owners while serving your community."

Andi hadn't put roots down deep enough yet to feel a real connection to the Gulf Springs community, but she certainly understood the concept of service. She also understood the value of networking. Still, she had enough on her plate right now without adding town politics.

"I moved here a little over two months ago. I would think you'd want someone more familiar with the town making decisions that impact its growth and direction."

"Longtime residents we've got. What we need is an infusion of new ideas and energy. We only meet once a month," the mayor cajoled. "Second Thursday, seven o'clock at the Elks Hall."

That was next week. Andi guessed what was coming before Al Frost issued the formal invitation.

"The meeting's open to the public. Why don't you stop by, watch your councilmen in action? Maybe they can convince you to join them."

"I've got a lot to do, but I guess I could poke my head in for a few minutes."

"Good enough."

Chair springs creaking, the mayor/used-car dealer rose and came around his desk to shake her hand.

"Whatever your decision and the outcome of my discussion with our attorney, I appreciate you bringing the matter to my attention. That's not how we want to do business in Gulf Springs."

WHEN SUE ELLEN STOPPED by on her way home from work later that evening, Andi had already fixed on two possible store-opening dates and zinged an e-mail off to Roger Brent. While intermittently checking her computer for a reply, she filled S.E. in on the sting.

"Darn! I wish I'd been there. I would have loved to see you and Dave go at it, even if it was for the camera."

Shedding her suit jacket, the blonde kicked off her stiletto heels and dropped into a chair. The overhead lights glinted on the satiny sheen of her panty hose as she swung both legs over the chair arm.

Andi decided then and there that one of the biggest benefits of being her own boss was the freedom to set her own dress code. With a little skill and cunning, she'd never have to skinny into another pair of panty hose.

"You have to show me that tape," Sue Ellen pleaded.

"I will."

After she'd edited out the sequence where she'd paid the interest on Dave's two hundred. She wasn't ready to explain the lip-lock to Sue Ellen.

She distracted her friend with a bag of Cheetos and a chuckle. "You're not going to believe what happened when I played the video for the mayor."

"He offered you a job as chief of police?" S.E. said around a mouthful of cheese curls.

"Close. He asked me to fill an empty seat on the town council."

"Good grief! You didn't agree, did you?"

"Not exactly."

"What does that mean?"

"It means I agreed to attend the next meeting and see how they operate."

"Oh, Andi, don't let them suck you in. I work with elected officials every day on some labor issue or another. Trust me, you don't want to get involved in small-town politics."

"The mayor made some valid points, Sue Ellen. If I'm going to live and run a business in Gulf Springs, I should give back to the community."

"What's to give back? You haven't taken anything *out* of the community yet."

"I will—or hope I will—as soon as I open my shop doors."

Excitement bubbled again. Reaching over, Andi plunged into the bag of Cheetos and grabbed a handful.

"I'm putting in my initial book order tomorrow. This time next week I'll be up to my ears in boxes and ISBNs."

"What's an is-ben?"

"Shorthand for International Standard Book Number. It's a ten- or thirteen-digit number bar-coded on the cover that identifies the book title, publisher and recommended retail price. I'll use it to manage my sales and inventory."

"Have you decided on your grand opening date yet?"

"I'm looking at the second Saturday in October, with the third Saturday as a fallback."

"Yikes! That's less than a month away. Will you be ready by then?"

"I'll have to be." She paused for dramatic effect. "If Roger Brent is available. If not, the date might slip."

Sue Ellen popped upright. "*The* Roger Brent? Author of *Blood Sport* and *Death Squad* and *Tango Sierra?* He's coming for your grand opening?"

"I hope so."

"How the heck did you pull that off?"

"I didn't. Chief Goodwin did. Which reminds me—I promised you'd be nice to him, Sue Ellen."

"Brent or Goodwin?"

"Goodwin."

"Ugh."

"Just look over his paperwork, okay? Expedite it if possible."

Sue Ellen mumbled something about crusty old farts with more push than pull but grudgingly agreed.

"You're going to have to hump to be ready by October, girl."

"Tell me about it! The next critical item on my agenda is to interview the part-timer I told you about. If she's still interested and available, I'm going to have her start when the books come in. The two of us should be able to scan and shelve the whole order in a few days."

"I can help."

"I appreciate the offer, but you already have a full-time job."

"So? You can't cut me out now. I'm having almost as much fun as you are, even if it's vicarious."

"I have no intention of cutting you out. In fact, if you're not too tired, I was hoping to bounce some ideas off you on ways to advertise the grand opening."

"Bounce away."

One silk-clad leg swinging, Sue Ellen crunched down Cheetos while Andi laid out her PR plan.

"If Brent can make the opening, I'm home free. Joe— Chief Goodwin—thinks his publisher will run radio and TV promos. If not, I'll try for another local author. I've already reserved ad space in the local and base newspapers. Since I'm catering to a largely military population, I thought the ads could include a discount coupon for anyone with a military ID."

"Oh, that's good. Everyone clips coupons these days."

Andi restrained a hoot. She doubted Sue Ellen Carson had ever clipped a coupon in her life.

"I also plan to print up flyers and do a bulk mailing."

"How much does that cost?"

"A bunch, but I feel better about mailing out flyers

than hiring kids to distribute them door-to-door. There are too many crazies out there."

"True." Catlike, Sue Ellen licked orange goo from her fingers. "Hey, I have an idea. Why don't we work the air show at Pensacola Naval Air Station? We could buy a booth and hand out the flyers there."

Andi had seen the TV and newspaper spots for the upcoming air show but hadn't thought to link it to her grand opening. She grasped the possibilities immediately, along with the problems.

"Booths at air shows are usually reserved for on-base activities like the Scouts or the photography club."

"Usually," S.E. agreed, "but not always. Defense contractors like Boeing or Raytheon always buy space to display their latest ray guns or hovercrafts. You may not be in the same category as the big guys, but you're providing a service to the military community. Or maybe you could link to an on-base activity like the library."

"Maybe."

"Come on, Colonel. You of all people should know how to work the system."

Andi squirmed, uncomfortable with the idea of manipulating any system or using her rank for personal gain. Still, she had to remember she was in business now, out to make a buck like everyone else in the civilian world.

"I'll check into it."

"Do that. Crash says the Blue Angels are performing at the air show. They always draw a monster crowd."

"Sounds like you and Major Steadman are conversing on a regular basis these days."

"I promised to call him back after my mad dash to the ER last night," Sue Ellen said with a shrug. "We stayed on the line for a while."

"Define *while*."

"An hour, maybe less."

"Oh, reeee-lly?"

"Yes, really. By the way, care to explain why your former husband had his hands under your hospital gown when I walked in?"

"Never mind the diversionary tactics. Tell me about you and Crash."

"There isn't much to tell. I called. We talked. He invited me to a dining out at Whiting Field next week."

Chewing on the inside of her cheek, Andi weighed her friendship with Sue Ellen against the one and only time Bill Steadman had opened up about the accident that had claimed his wife. His grief—and raw, searing guilt—had stayed with Andi for weeks afterward.

"You know Bill's a widower, right?"

"Yes, you told me. I mentioned something about his wife the other night, when we were here for dinner. He sort of shut down on me."

"He took her death hard."

"So you said. And obviously still isn't over it. That's okay. I'm not looking for a deep, meaningful relationship with him or anyone else."

"What are you looking for?"

"Sex, girl, sex. The raunchier the better." Stretching her legs, Sue Ellen wiggled her nylon-covered toes back and forth. "Looks like I'll have to sit through a long, boring dining out before I have my way with the boy, but I suspect he'll be worth it."

"Clearly you've never attended a helo squadron dining out. Long and boring they ain't."

"Mmm."

Loot in anticipation of a possible postparty orgy, S.E. contemplated her toes.

Andi, in turn, contemplated her friend. She and Sue Ellen had been as close as sisters for more than ten years and had seen each other through some very rough patches. Yet she'd worked with Crash and knew how deep his scars went. She hoped she wasn't setting either of her friends up for another fall.

With another lazy stretch, Sue Ellen broke into her thoughts. "So tell me. What *were* Dave's hands doing under your hospital gown last night?"

CHAPTER 12

The e-mail from Roger Brent was waiting in the laptop's in-box when Andi got up the next morning. Yes, he was available the second Saturday in October. Even better, his publisher had agreed to an early release of his new hardback, *Return to Aravanche*, to coincide with his appearance.

Whooping, Andi danced through the entire house before putting in a call to Chief Goodwin. She must have dragged him out of the shower, as she could hear water splashing in the background. At least she hoped it was the water. With Special Tactics, you never knew.

"Joe! It's Andi. Brent's a go. *Thank you*."

"You're welcome. When's he coming over?"

"Saturday, October eleventh, from eleven to one."

"I should be able to make it. If not, don't forget my autographed copy."

"I won't."

Fired by an enthusiasm and energy she hadn't felt in years, Andi jumped into action. That same morning she dashed off e-mails and followed up with calls to her Ingram distributor.

After placing her initial book order, she wrote ad copy, designed flyers and called the sign maker to order a banner announcing her grand opening, which he promised to deliver with the shop sign. With those critical actions completed, she worked the phones and Internet to notify various chambers of commerce of her grand opening. She kept so busy over the next few days she almost forgot her regularly scheduled blood test and had to dash over to Hurlburt to get it done on the run.

In the midst of this whirlwind of activity she hired her first and only employee. Andi had met Karen Duchek at a dark and somewhat dank used bookstore specializing in horror and occult. Karen was bright and bubbly, with a generous set of curves to match her smile. She'd confessed that she found some of the customers just a little strange and was ready for a change in employment.

Andi arranged for them to meet at the shop at nine-thirty. Deciding she needed to look at least semibusiness-like, she traded her jeans and tank top for a short-sleeved cotton sweater in dusty rose, drawstring slacks in a darker pink and beaded flip-flops. Her hair had grown enough to sweep up in a twist and anchor with a clip.

She had coffee and a selection of gooey delights from the doughnut hut down the street waiting when the mother of two pulled up in a dinged minivan. Andi had reviewed her résumé and had already decided to hire her, but Karen sealed the deal with the first word out of her mouth.

"Wow!"

Jaw sagging, the gingery redhead performed a slow pirouette. Andi swallowed a silly lump of pride as she viewed her creation through the younger woman's eyes.

Light poured through the plate glass window. Feathery palms and ficuses formed inviting alcoves for the chairs and computer stations scattered around the shop. Rack after rack of bookshelves stood ready and waiting.

Karen spun in a circle, her buttercup-yellow skirt billowing above her ankle socks and Mary Janes. "This place is fabulous. *Please* tell me you haven't hired all the help you need."

"I haven't. How about some coffee and doughnuts while we talk?"

"Yes to both."

Chocolate-glazed in hand, Andi flipped open the file she'd begun on Karen. As yet, all it included was the résumé the young wife had e-mailed and a blank employment form Andi had copied off the Internet.

"You've racked up quite a bit of experience in the book business. Part-time at your local library all through high school. Volunteer at your kids' school library four hours a week. Three years at the used bookstore."

"I've always loved books. My earliest memory is sitting on my mom's lap while she rocked me and read *The Little Engine That Could*."

"'I think I can, I think I can, I think I can,'" Andi quoted, smiling. "That was one of my favorites, too."

"Both of my boys will recite the entire book, line for line, at the least provocation. I read it to them until the pages shredded."

"I like that you've taken some business and marketing courses at the community college. You're certainly highly qualified. I'm curious, though. Why do you want to work in a small shop when one of the big chains would probably snap you up in a heartbeat?"

"The nearest big chain is a good twenty miles from my house. I need be close to home when one of the boys takes a dive off the parallel bars at school and breaks a leg."

"Does that happen often?"

"Often enough. I won't kid you, Colonel Armstrong. My boys are, well, adventurous."

Andi gave her high marks for honesty.

"We'll work around any catastrophes at school. And, please, call me Andi."

The woman nodded but looked uncomfortable with that last bit. As the wife of a staff sergeant stationed at Hurlburt Field, she would understand and respect the invisible barriers of rank.

Now for the tricky part. Andi wouldn't ask anyone to work in close proximity to her without disclosing the reason for her abrupt departure from active duty. She'd considered and discarded a dozen different approaches. Finally she settled on the most direct.

"Before we proceed any further, I think you should know I brought an uninvited guest home with me from Iraq. A stubborn little bug known as *acinetobacter baumannii*. The troops call it Saddam's Revenge."

To her relief, her potential employee didn't recoil in alarm.

"I've heard about that," Karen said slowly. "One of the men in my husband's squadron was hit by small-arms fire during a raid in Basra. The wound got infected with this bug. It's still in his system." The young wife's brow knit. "It lives in the sand, doesn't it? Desert sand?"

"That's what they tell me, although variations are supposedly present in the soil in every part of the world, even here."

Andi feathered her fingers across her chin. The scar was almost invisible under a light layer of makeup.

"The docs say the bacteria reside harmlessly on the skin. Once this particular strain gets into the blood, though, it's tough to root out. They don't as yet know why it's proving so resistant to antibiotics."

"But it's not contagious?"

"Again, that's what they tell me."

"I guess they'd quarantine folks if it was."

"I guess so. Do you want to take some time to think about this or talk to your husband before we discuss the specifics of the job?"

Karen downed a doughnut while she mulled that over.

"No," she announced after a moment, "I'm good with it. Jerry—my husband—works alongside that troop who took the hit. He hasn't caught the bug. Nobody in the squadron has. But…"

"What?"

She nibbled on her lower lip. "The odds are I might pass something on to *you*. My kids always bring whatever's going around home from school."

"We don't have to worry about that. I'm taking enough antibiotics to kick the bubonic plague in the butt."

Relieved that touchy subject was behind them, Andi made the offer. "If you want the job, I can start you at eight-fifty an hour."

"Eight-fifty? Are you serious?"

"I know it's only two dollars above minimum wage, but we can renegotiate after—"

"I'll take it, I'll take it!"

With an embarrassed laugh, Karen explained her eagerness. "I haven't been earning anything *close* to minimum wage. You know how it is. A military wife walks in looking for a job, potential bosses know her husband could get orders any day. They don't want to hire and train someone who might have to quit the next month. When you add two young kids and a need for flexible hours to the equation, you're lucky if they'll even talk to you."

"Well, I sincerely hope your husband doesn't get orders for a while. I'd love for you to help me launch this shop."

"When do you want me to start?"

"As soon as possible. How much notice do you have to give at your other job?"

Her mouth curved in a sheepish grin. "I gave notice the day after we talked. I was hoping you'd hire me. If you didn't, I would have quit anyway. One of the customers walked in sporting a bloody dagger dangling from a chain around his neck. He really creeped me out."

"He would creep me out, too. Let's hope he doesn't decide to shop here."

"Are you going to carry horror?"

"Some. I want to cater to all readers, of course, but my analyses indicate the bulk of our customers will be military—active, retired, reserve."

Dragging her hefty op plan across the counter, Andi flipped to the tab containing local population statistics.

A bar graph with stair-stepping green columns summarized her weeks of data gathering.

"The tourist trade should account for our next largest customer base. Then women. Publishing industry statistics indicate they're the most avid readers. Then children and young adults."

She dropped an acetate overlay onto the population chart. Bright orange lines bisected the green bars at various points.

"For the military base, we'll stock up on men's action-adventures, thrillers, war novels and military history."

Casually she dropped the name of the author who'd agreed to come in for the grand opening. Karen almost fell off her stool.

"Omigod! Wait until Jerry hears about this! He *loves* Roger Brent. He and every troop in his squadron will line up for a signed copy."

Andi let her gush for several minutes before returning to the charts. "For the tourists, we'll stock up on a variety of paperback bestsellers they can take to the beach, as well as travel guides and books with local interest. Female readers go for mystery and bestsellers, too, but I've ordered a full line of books by top romance authors. I'm hoping you'll review the children's selections and make any changes you think necessary."

Karen studied the fat binder with a combination of

awe and trepidation. "I'll be happy to make suggestions, but I'm not sure I can lay them out with such…such precise detail."

"Not to worry." Andi chuckled. "I tend to go a little overboard on spreadsheets. Between my analytical approach to this business and your in-store smarts, we should make a heck of a team."

Pleasure colored the younger woman's face almost the same shade as her terra cotta hair. "Thanks, Colonel. Uh, Andi."

"Why don't I show you around the shop?"

Karen oohed over the reading alcoves and gave grateful thanks for the microwave and fridge in the store-room at the rear of the shop.

"I'm doing Lean Cuisine these days. Most of the time," she amended, obviously remembering the sugary dough-nuts. "Jerry says he likes having more of me to love, but I'm tired of shopping for tents instead of dresses."

To Andi's delight, her new employee proved her worth not two minutes later. After surveying the area intended for the children's section, Karen recommended a slight rearrangement of the bookshelves.

"If we angle them a little, we could make a play space back in this corner. Maybe add a carpet for toddlers to crawl on and some child-size chairs. And, if possible, you might think about another computer terminal for this space. Or a small TV with a Game Boy. The kids can play video games while Mom and Dad browse."

"That's a wonderful idea."

Andi could have kicked herself for not thinking of it herself. The last time she'd visited D.C.'s largest mall, she'd been both amazed and amused by the hordes of two- and three-year-olds pounding keyboards at the Apple store.

"I should to be able to spring for another used computer. Why don't we ask your boys to recommend some games? Ones they'd like to play if you get in a crunch and have to bring them in with you."

Karen did a double take. "You mean you don't mind me bringing the boys to work?"

"I wouldn't want you to do it on a regular basis, but I spent twenty-one years in uniform. I know your husband's life isn't his own. Yours, either, when it comes to short-notice TDYs and deployments. If you do bring the boys in, though, make them *promise* to refrain from diving off the shelves and breaking legs."

"I will."

Just in case, Andi thought, she'd better make sure she didn't leave any sharp tools or box cutters lying around the storeroom. She'd also check her insurance policy. She'd purchased a million in liability and enough personal property to cover her investment. That *should* take care of all contingencies, including two active boys.

"So when do you want me to start?" Karen asked again after the tour.

"How about tomorrow? I'm expecting my first ship-ment of books. You can help me scan them in and shelve them."

"Tomorrow's good. The boys are in school from eight to three-fifteen. I can stay that whole day if you need me."

They were working out a schedule for the next two weeks when a truck pulled up to the shop.

"Finally! The sign for above the front door."

Karen's excitement mirrored Andi's as the two women stood on the sidewalk and watched the installation crew mount the backlit plastic sign. When the crew peeled away the protective adhesive covering to reveal the sand-colored lettering set against a vivid turquoise backdrop, Karen voiced enthusiastic approval.

"A Great Read. It's simple yet enthusiastic. The perfect name for a bookstore."

Andi had to agree. She'd considered and discarded hundreds of names, including the more exotic ones sug-gested by S.E. and Crash. In the end she'd gone with one she thought conveyed exactly what her shop was all about.

"Oh, look at that logo," Karen exclaimed when the installers peeled away the last of the adhesive backing. "I love it!"

Andi did, too, especially since she'd designed it herself. She'd wanted to capture the essence of the unspoiled beaches surrounding Gulf Springs. Hence the turquoise and sand colors, the hint of dunes and feathery sea oats in the logo and the stack of books waiting beside an open beach umbrella.

Not exactly James Bond or Scarlett O'Hara. Yet the longer Andi gazed at the sign, the more *right* it felt.

Her fellow entrepreneurs seemed to agree. The manager of the beachwear shop on her left came out to admire the sign and inquire about the kinds of books she planned to stock. The cook and the waitress working the seafood restaurant across the street joined the small crowd. Even the pharmacist from the drugstore on the corner strolled down for a look-see.

Their warm welcome and promises to hand out flyers in their establishments announcing her grand opening left Andi feeling buoyed and more excited than ever.

STILL BASKING IN THE glow, she hung around the shop until dusk to test the sign's illumination. She made her first observation from the middle of the road. When both the logo and the shop name showed beautifully from that vantage point, she walked up one side of the street and down the other. Only after she was satisfied she could spot A Great Read from almost any angle did she lock up and drive home.

The light spilling through the windows of Dave's place tugged at her like a bungee cord. She hadn't seen or talked to him since the sting. His house had been dark when she'd arrived home the past few nights.

She'd picked up the phone to call him a couple of times. Once to tell him about the mayor's offer of a seat on the town council, once to ask when she could return the camcorder. On both occasions she'd snapped down the lid of her cell phone before the call went through.

They needed time. Correction—*she* needed time. Dave seemed determined to pick up where they'd left off, but she hadn't been prepared for his unexpected reappearance in her life. Still less for the wild emotions that rocketed through her with every kiss.

She could understand the heat. Whatever else they'd messed up, Dave had always known just how to key her ignition switch and vice versa. They probably set several world records their first few years, going from fully dressed to naked in four-point-five seconds or less.

The urge to strip and straddle him was still there and growing fiercer with each passing day. Problem was, Andi wasn't sure what she wanted to follow the stripping and straddling. They'd jumped out of bed and into marriage once. Older and wiser, she was determined to look before she leaped this time around.

Her rented house welcomed her like the friend it was fast becoming. Kicking off her flip-flops, Andi curled her toes into the smooth satin of the kitchen tiles and plopped her purse on the kitchen counter. The op plan thudded down beside it. With the memory of her trip to the ER still fresh in her mind, she made for the fridge.

No more skipped meals for this girl.

The champagne Sue Ellen had brought occupied place of honor on the top shelf. Tonight would have been a great time to pop the cork, Andi thought, to toast the hiring of her first employee and the great sign hanging.

She had to share the thrill of those events. Carrying the makings for a salad to the sink, she punched Sue Ellen's speed-dial number.

"Hey, y'all," S.E.'s digitized recording chirped in her ear. "Leave a message."

"It's Andi. I need to talk to you. Call me when you get home and we'll… Oh, wait. I forgot. Tonight's the big dining out at Whiting Field, isn't it? *Definitely* call me. I want a full report."

She was munching her way through spinach greens

and a grilled chicken breast when the phone shrilled. It was too early for Sue Ellen to render a report unless she was calling from the dining out.

But it could be Dave. He may have seen her lights.

Her pulse leaping, Andi grabbed the phone and checked caller ID. The USAF clinic at Hurlburt. Fighting a sharp stab of disappointment, she hit Talk.

"Colonel Armstrong."

"Good evening, Colonel. This is Dr. Ramirez."

"You're working late this evening, Doc. No soccer game tonight?"

"Not tonight. I've been reviewing the results of your latest blood test and thought I should call you."

A groan formed deep in Andi's chest. Oh, God! Not now. Not again. She'd just started to rebuild her world. Was it going to come crashing down around her again? She held her breath, awaiting the verdict.

"Looks like the mix of antibiotics you're taking has done the trick. Your blood shows no trace of *acineto-bacter baumannii*."

Relief exploded through her in bright, happy starbursts. "For real?"

"For real."

The flight surgeon let her revel in the results for a few moments.

"This doesn't mean you're home free. That strain of

bacteria has proved incredibly resilient. We need to continue to check your blood and your heart for at least another six months."

"No problem. What about the antibiotics? Should I stay with them?"

"I've got you on a pretty powerful cocktail. Let's stop the Amikacin and cut the Polymixin B to half. We'll reassess dosage after your next checkup."

Her reference to cocktails reminded Andi of the champagne in the fridge. "I'm in the mood to celebrate. Is it safe to down a glass of bubbly?"

"A glass or two won't hurt. Have one for me."

"I will. Thanks for the call, Doc."

"You're welcome."

Andi hip-hopped all the way to the fridge. With a few simple words the flight surgeon had blasted away the ugly black cloud that had been hanging over her almost half a year now. What a perfect ending to an already incredible day!

Except she wasn't ready for it to end. She wanted to share her news.

She thought about calling her sister. Carol had been so shaken by the realization that her rock, the lifeline she'd clung to during those awful years of addiction, now had demons of her own to deal with. She'd begged Andi to come home to Ohio and promised to nurse her day and night, which would have driven them both nutso within a week.

The shiny gold foil capping the Piper-Heidsieck decided the matter. She'd call Carol later. This news demanded in-person, in-the-flesh celebrating.

Snagging the champagne, Andi wiggled her feet into her flip-flops and sailed out the side door.

CHAPTER 13

Dave opened the front door and felt his insides lurch sideways.

Andi stood on the stoop, her eyes glowing like backlit emeralds in the porch lights. He needed only one look at her face, just one, to acknowledge he'd bend steel with his bare hands to keep this woman in his life.

Grinning, she hefted a dew-streaked bottle. "I come bearing gifts."

"So I see."

"Care to join me in a snort?"

"Sure."

When she waltzed into the foyer, Dave kick-started his heart and closed the door. Good thing he'd delayed his run. He might have missed her, although he would have preferred to greet her in something other than biker shorts and an airflow tank with oversize armholes.

She, on the other hand, looked good enough to eat in a pink cotton top and drawstring slacks. He liked the way she'd drawn back her hair with that plastic clip, exposing the clean line of her jaw and throat. Liked even more the idea of tugging the clip loose and burying his face in the silky mass. Battling the urge, he ushered her down the hall.

"What are we celebrating?"

"I'll tell you when you pop the cork."

She sashayed past him. A second later she stopped dead on the steps leading down into the living area that ran the full length of the house.

"This is fabulous!"

With a small jolt Dave realized this was her first incursion inside his home. She hadn't made it past the front door the night she'd come to check out possible crack dealers.

"I love all the open space," she breathed, taking in the continuous flow from kitchen to dining area to great room. "And the way the architect used columns and recessed ceilings to separate the areas visually."

He could tell just when the realization hit her. Her brows drew together. Her head cocked. Frowning, she made another sweep.

"This looks a lot like the home we talked about building someday."

"It should. I had it designed with that open floor plan in mind."

"Well," she said after a small, awkward pause, "now we know the design works."

"Yeah, it does."

Dave didn't figure this was the time to admit he'd instructed the architect to follow Andi's specific layout for her dream kitchen. Or that memories of the cramped bathrooms they'd steamed up on four continents had dictated the oversize shower in the master bedroom.

"Mind if I explore?" she asked.

"Go ahead. I'll open the champagne."

While Dave detoured to the walk-in bar, she roamed the great room. He wasn't surprised when the collection of photos decorating one wall snagged her attention. Hooking her thumbs on the pockets of her silky slacks, she studied the eclectic mix of landscapes, deployment scenes and family mug shots.

Dave, in turn, studied the way her shoulders arched and stretched the front of her pink top across her breasts. His gut tightening, he remembered how perfectly those soft mounds had fit his palms. Remembered, too, how the nipples had stiffened to proud, dusky tips when he'd worked them with his tongue and teeth and…

"Oh, Lord! I can't believe you framed this picture."

Wrenching his attention upward, he saw her grimacing at a picture of the two of them in wet suits and face masks. They'd just surfaced after a dive off the North Carolina coast and had mugged for the camera, giving excellent imitations of pop-eyed, puff-cheeked blowfish.

"That's one of my favorites." His thumbs worked the cork. "It was your first dual-tank dive, remember?"

"What I remember is swallowing half the Atlantic before I got my regulator working properly."

She leaned closer to peer at another photo and treated Dave to a primo view of her rear. Gritting his teeth, he shot the cork into the air.

The pop brought her upright—thank God! Ambling over to the bar, she perched on a swivel stool while Dave slid two tall pilsner glasses from the overhead rack. His taste in barware didn't run to expensive crystal champagne flutes. He'd insisted Andi keep those, along with their Waterford wine goblets and brandy snifters.

Carrying the pilsner glasses around the counter, he handed her one and hitched a hip on the stool next to hers. "Okay, what are we toasting?"

"Nothing much," she said with a smug smile. "Just the sign that went up today officially designating my shop as A Great Read."

"Congratulations."

Clinking glasses, they tipped the champagne to their lips. Andi took a delicate sip. Dave downed a healthy swallow. The bubbles were still fizzing in his nostrils when her smile widened into a grin.

"*And* I hired an employee this morning."

"Double congratulations."

They clinked again.

"*And* Roger Brent agreed to a book signing during my grand opening."

"Joe mentioned he was working on Brent. Glad they came through for you."

Andi downed another sip but obviously had more news to share. Excitement blazed in her face and had her almost squirming on her stool. Amused, Dave played straight man for her.

"Okay, Armstrong. Spill it. What else are we celebrating?"

"Dr. Ramirez called a little while ago."

Okay, he told himself. All right. No need to panic. It had to be good news. She wouldn't be wearing that silly grin otherwise. Still, the best he could push out was a growl.

"I need another 'and' here."

"And my latest blood test came back clean. The doc said they found no trace of my nasty little hitchhiker. None. Nada. Nixola."

"Sierra Hotel!"

Slamming down his glass, he shoved off his stool, scooped Andi from hers and tossed her into the air. Champagne sprayed in all directions.

"Dave!"

Half laughing, half shrieking, she dropped into his arms and went airborne again.

"Stop! This is my first taste of alcohol in five months! I'm already half sloshed."

"I vote we go for one hundred percent."

He let her slide to her feet and reached behind her to replenish her depleted supply.

"Here's to you, babe."

Dave didn't bother to refill his own glass. Keeping her in a loose hold, he tilted the bottle to his mouth. He couldn't remember the last time he'd had a buzz on—or had something this momentous to celebrate.

Andi's glass didn't make the return trip to her lips. She hadn't exaggerated. She was already light-headed. Watching Dave guzzle Sue Ellen's expensive Piper-Heidsieck kicked the whirling sensation up several notches.

His head tipped back to expose the strong line of his jaw. His throat worked, cording the sinew. Valiantly Andi battled the insane impulse to lean in and nip his flesh. Then hunger and need got all mixed up with the wild exhilaration still singing in her veins.

One bite. That's all it took. Dave froze for two, maybe three, seconds. The next thing Andi knew, he'd abandoned the champagne and banded her against him. She saw her hunger mirrored in his burning blue eyes.

"You're half a heartbeat away from naked," he warned

in a low growl. "If you want me to back off, speak now or forever hold your peace."

Andi was too far gone to heed the *forever* bit. Her senses were exploding in bright pinpoints of heat. Every nerve in her body now screamed for more.

For this one night, this one hour, she could dump the worry she'd carried around for so many months. She could stop analyzing, stop trying to figure out where she and Dave were headed, stop weighing their past mistakes against a hazy future. She could stop thinking altogether, she decided fiercely, and just *feel*.

"Naked sounds pretty good right now, Armstrong."

The husky admission had barely left her lips before he had his hands under the hem of her cotton sweater. His calloused palms planed upward. Quivering under his touch, Andi raised her arms.

"I've missed this." Dropping hard, fast kisses on her mouth, Dave dragged the sweater over her head. "The feel of you. The taste of you."

He had her bare to the waist when Andi reciprocated by attacking his tank. Loose and baggy for airflow, it came off with one swift tug.

Oh, God, she'd missed him, too. Her hands slicked over his shoulders, down his back. In a frenzy of need, she locked her mouth on his and burrowed under the waistband of his running shorts. The black Lycra gave easily, and his jockstrap presented only a momentary obstacle. Dragging both down, she curved her hands over his taut butt and kneaded the smooth flesh.

His breath hissed out. She could feel him go stiff and erect against her belly. She squeezed again, loving the power, loving the wild sensations racing through her. Loving him.

The last thought arrowed through her sensual haze, but before she had time to process it, Dave jerked back a few inches. His breath fast and rough, he yanked on the drawstring of her slacks. The silky fabric slithered over her hips. Almost before it pooled around her ankles, he'd backed her against the wall.

He used one hand to anchor her wrists above her head. The other wedged between their bodies. Dragging aside the elastic of her panties, he fingered her slick flesh. The heel of his hand applied an exquisite unrelenting pressure.

Gasping, Andi hooked a leg over his hip to give him freer access. He took advantage of it to slide two fingers inside her. Head back, neck arched, she let him work the magic he'd always worked.

She'd intended to take for just a few moments. Ride this pleasure only a minute or two before returning it.

She'd counted without Dave's skill. Keeping her pinned to the wall, he used his hands and his mouth and his tongue to devastating effect. Tight, hot swirls built in her belly. She could feel the climax rushing at her with every spasm of her vaginal muscles.

"Wait, Dave! It's been too long. I'm too…too—damn!"

The swirls exploded into white heat. A groan ripped from her throat. Eyes squeezed tight, Andi let the waves crash through her.

Dave held her while she floated back to Earth. Her lids fluttered up. The smug male triumph on his face brought a grin to hers.

"You always were good with your hands, Armstrong."

"You think so, huh?" Grinning, he scooped her up again and strode toward what she assumed was the bedroom. "Wait till you see my fancy new footwork."

BY THE TIME ANDI RESURFACED yet again, she'd gained a new respect for all twenty of Dave's digits. Limp and slick with sweat, she squirmed under the weight of the arm he'd flung across her middle.

"Tell me again about Doc Ramirez's call." His deep voice dragged her from semiconsciousness. "The full version this time."

"She said my blood showed no trace of the bacteria and adjusted my mix of antibiotics."

"How long does she want you to take them?"

"Until my next checkup at least." Rolling onto her side, she nuzzled his throat. "She also said I wasn't home free, that I needed to continue the blood work and cardiac workups for another six months."

He stroked her hair, digesting that. "Then what?" he asked quietly.

"Then," Andi mumbled into the warm skin of his neck, "I don't know."

"Think you might apply to go back on active duty?"

Two months ago her answer would have been instant and automatic. Shell-shocked by her abrupt retirement, Andi would have jumped at the chance to return to military service. Even as little as two weeks ago she might have pushed for a medical evaluation board at the earliest possible date.

Except two weeks ago she hadn't wrested a permit from a crooked building inspector. Or ordered almost eight thousand dollars worth of stock. Or hired an employee and watched an installation crew hang her shop sign.

Or tumbled into bed with her ex-husband.

She could undo everything but that, Andi realized. Wiggling out from under his arm, she levered up onto an elbow. Her tangled hair tumbled to her shoulders and enclosed her and Dave in a dark cocoon. After what had just happened between them, she owed him an honest answer.

"I don't know what I'm going to do. I thought I'd miss

the responsibility, the adrenaline rush, the sense of being part of something really important. I also wasn't sure how I'd function outside the military environment, seeing as it's all I've ever known. Yet these past weeks I've been discovering there *is* life after the Air Force."

"That's what they tell me."

"It's true. There's another world out there, Dave. One that isn't fueled by sixteen-hour days and doesn't require decisions impacting thousands of lives. It's smaller than the world I was used to but incredibly exhilarating. I'm not sure I want to give it up—or trade my jeans and flip-flops for boots and BDUs again."

"Tough decision," he agreed, curling a strand around his thumb. "Do I get a vote?"

Again she hesitated. "Maybe. In six months, when it comes to crunch time."

His eyes locked with hers. "Six months is a long time to just hang loose."

"Gimme a break, Armstrong! You were hardly hanging loose a few minutes ago."

Laughter rumbled around in his chest. "No, I guess I wasn't."

Propping her chin on her hand, Andi trailed a finger through the swirls of hair on his chest. "You, me…us. I feel as though we've taken another right oblique. I'm not sure *what* direction we're marching in now."

"We'll figure it out."

And it wouldn't take any six months, Dave vowed fiercely. Tugging on the strand of dark hair, he brought her mouth down to his.

PALE STREAKS OF LIGHT filtered through the shutters when a buzz jerked Andi from a deep sleep. The mattress tilted as Dave propped himself up on one elbow and fumbled for the phone on the nightstand.

"Armstrong."

His bulk formed a formidable shield but didn't block Sue Ellen's anxious voice.

"I can't reach Andi. She left me a message last night, said she needed to talk to me. I've been calling since I got home a little while ago, but she doesn't answer her house or cell phone. Have you heard from her? She's not in the hospital, is she?"

"No, she's not."

"Do you know where she is?"

Dave angled around and caught Andi's eye. A wicked grin stretched his mouth. "Matter of fact, I do."

The mattress sagged again as he rolled over to offer Andi the phone. Shaking her head, she dragged the sheet up over her face. Fiendishly Dave peeled it back.

"It's Sue Ellen," he announced with wholly unnecessary glee.

"I'll get you for this, Armstrong."

Andi took the phone and decided a swift offense was her best defense. "Did I hear you say you just got home? That must have been some dining out."

She should have known she couldn't throw Sue Ellen off stride that easily. After a mere second or two of startled silence, her friend counterattacked in her own inimitable style.

"It *was* a great dining out," she purred. "What came after was even better. Say hello to Crash."

Andi's jaw sagged. A few seconds later Bill Steadman's amused voice greeted her.

"Hi, Andi."

"Hi, Crash."

Surprise flickered across Dave's face, followed by a slow, feral smile Andi had no difficulty interpreting.

"Good to know you're not stretched out dead on your kitchen floor," Crash drawled.

S.E. sniggered in the background. "Ask her where she *is* stretched out."

Thankfully Bill ignored that. "Sue Ellen turned a little frantic when she couldn't reach you," he said instead. "We both did."

"I'm, uh, fine."

That produced another snigger and brought Sue Ellen back on the line. "I'm guessing you're a damn sight better than fine this morning, girl. To echo your own words, I want a full report."

The ridiculousness of the situation erased Andi's chagrin at being caught in her ex-husband's bed.

"I'll give you one," she promised, laughing. "*After* I hear yours."

"Deal. I'll swing by your place after work tonight."

"Speaking of work…" Andi heard Crash say. This was followed by a shriek from Sue Ellen.

"Oh, God! Tell me it's not really seven-ten!"

Evidently it was, as her friend hurriedly terminated the call. "Gotta hit the shower. Later, girl."

Still chuckling, Andi passed the phone back to Dave. "Sounds like last night was full of surprises all around," she commented.

"That's a roger."

When he reached over to deposit the phone on the nightstand, Andi couldn't resist gliding her fingers over the plane of his back. As light as it was, the touch stirred something deep and almost forgotten inside her.

How many times had a phone or alarm jerked them from sleep? How often had she longed to snuggle into Dave's warmth for another ten or fifteen minutes before hitting the shower and pulling on her uniform?

Why *hadn't* they snatched a few quiet moments to anchor their day instead of springing out of bed and into their frenetic routines? Quietly grieving for all those lost opportunities, Andi attempted to extricate herself from the tangled sheets.

"You need to get to work. Your exec is probably forming a search party by now."

"I called him earlier, while you were still asleep. Told him I'd be in later." As if he'd read her mind, Dave tugged her down beside him and settled her in the crook of his arm. "Tell me what's on your agenda today."

"It's not as full as yours, I'm sure, but I'll stay busy. I'm expecting my first shipment of books this morning. Karen Duchek, my new assistant, said she'd come in to help scan and shelve them."

Excitement crept into her voice. She couldn't *wait* to crack open box after box of books and fill her empty shelves.

That was when Andi realized she'd already nudged close to one decision. Whatever the docs said six months from now, she'd have to think long and hard before she went back on active duty. She'd loved her old life, but the new one was opening exciting vistas for her.

Deciding to hug her thoughts to herself until she had time to sort through their implications, she filled Dave in on the rest of her schedule. "This afternoon, my seventeen-year-old computer wiz is installing another terminal for the kids' corner."

His fingers combed lazily through her hair. "Kids' corner?"

"That was Karen's idea. Oh, and the Gulf Springs town council meets tonight. I promised the mayor I'd stop by for a little while. I'd better call Sue Ellen and re-schedule our reporting session."

Her mind buzzed with all she had to do, yet Andi didn't feel the least inclination to jump out of bed and get to it. The slow rise and fall of Dave's chest was almost as seductive as the hunger that had literally driven them against the wall last night.

"What about you?" she asked. "What does the rest of your day look like?"

With a wry smile, he echoed her earlier reply. "I'll stay busy. Want to get together after your council meeting to compare notes and decompress?"

Angling her head, she looked into his eyes. This decision came easily and without hesitation.

"Sounds good to me, Armstrong."

CHAPTER 14

When UPS ground service delivered the first shipment of books, Andi felt as though Christmas had arrived three months early. Like a six-year-old who'd snuck downstairs to find presents heaped under the tree, she shivered in joyous anticipation.

Karen was every bit as eager. "Go ahead," she urged. "Open one."

Both women had dressed for a day of bending, lifting and shelving. Andi was in jeans and a baggy purple T-shirt with the JCS emblem emblazoned in gold across the front. Karen's hot-pink capris and matching smock made her hair look more orange than red, but their elastic waist and loose fit were designed for easy movement.

"Okay." Andi poised the blade of her box cutter over the first carton. "Here goes."

The blade sliced cleanly through paper tape. Eager hands folded back cardboard flaps to reveal neat stacks of paperback thrillers.

"Ooooh!" Squealing, Karen fell on the top one. "Nelson DeMille's latest. This is the first time I've seen it in softcover. I have to buy this for Jerry."

Two layers down she yelped again. "*I* want this Stuart Woods."

Andi had ordered only a few copies of each title, opting for variety instead of depth. As she lifted out the next layer, she began to suspect Karen might be her best customer.

"Good thing I get an employee discount," the young wife groaned. "Isn't that Patricia Cornwell's latest?"

"It is."

Andi fondled the cover with a combination of reverence and exultation. Books had always been her joy, her entertainment, her escape. Now they constituted her livelihood. She knew the more mundane aspects of running a business would eventually blunt the excitement of opening cartons of books, but right now, at this moment, she felt as though she'd raised the lid on a chest crammed with priceless treasures. Alive with the thrill of the moment, she slipped out the printed notice inserted in Cornwell's book.

"This indicates the official on-sale date isn't until next week."

"Good!" Greed laced her assistant's reply. "That gives us plenty of time to read it—so we can give our customers an honest recommendation," she tacked on.

"Of course."

Paperback in hand, Andi reached for the wireless scanner wand. She'd tested her computerized inventory-and-sales system a dozen or more times on books from her personal library. Now for the real thing.

"Ready?"

"Ready," Karen confirmed, squirming around for a clear view of the laptop perched atop another carton.

Both women held their breath as Andi aimed the wand at the bar code on the back cover. After a beep and a thin red beam, a string of data painted across the screen.

Karen let out a whoop of delight. "There it is! The very first entry from the very first carton of your very first shipment."

"*Our* very first shipment." Battling a ridiculous reluctance to let the paperback out of her hands, Andi set it aside. "One down, several thousand to go."

It didn't take long for the women to develop a smooth rhythm. One opened cartons and scanned, the other shelved. They alternated tasks at regular intervals throughout the morning, breaking only to snack on the Weight Watchers bars Karen had stuffed in her straw tote.

Andi hadn't forgotten her trip to the ER She kept an eye on the clock and was just about to call a halt for lunch when the waitress from the seafood restaurant across the street appeared with a large, steaming sack.

"We saw the UPS truck deliver all these boxes," the aproned brunette told Andi and Karen. "We—Sam and I—figured you two would be hard at it and might need something to keep you going. Sam's the cook," she added for clarification. "I'm Heather."

Touched by their kindness, Andi offered repayment in kind. "Thanks, Heather. And please thank Sam for us. If you'll tell me what kind of books you both like to read, I'll return the favor."

"I've got four kids," the waitress said with a chuckle. "I don't have time to read, but Sam eats up those *Death on Demand* books by Carol somebody."

"Carolyn Hart," Andi and Karen chorused.

Their instant and enthusiastic response made Heather blink in surprise.

"I *love* her books," Karen declared earnestly. "Especially those featuring the Darlings."

"Me, too." Andi added her endorsement to her assistant's. "I think Carolyn Hart is the greatest writer of traditional mysteries of our generation."

"If you say so. Gotta get back to work. Good luck with all these boxes."

Heather and Sam weren't the only ones who'd noticed the UPS truck. The owner of the beachwear shop next door also popped in to take a peek at Andi's stock and offer a word of warning about window displays.

"The afternoon sun hits this side of the street full blast. It'll fade the colors on these book jackets fast. You might want to buy a roll of stick-on window tint or have an awning installed."

"I can't believe I didn't think of that. Thanks for the advice."

AFTER A SMALL BREAK FOR lunch, the two women worked side by side until Karen had to head home to meet her boys' school bus. Sliding the blade of her box cutter into its plastic handle, she surveyed the stacks of unopened boxes.

"I hate to leave. We've hardly made a dent."

"I'd say fifteen cartons is more than a dent."

The young mother eyed the boxes once more, obviously reluctant to miss out on the treasures they contained. "You're not going to stay here all night and open the rest by yourself, are you?"

"Hardly. I have plans for tonight."

Those plans had flitted in and out of Andi's head all day, adding another fillip of excitement to the thrill of delving into her first shipment.

"I'll open a few more boxes, then I have to go home and clean up for a town council meeting."

Followed by another more intimate meeting.

Andi would make a brief appearance at the council as promised. She suspected her session with Dave would run considerably longer. She didn't have to work hard to figure out which of those prospects made her nipples tingle with anticipation.

With another reluctant glance at the waiting cartons, her assistant gathered her purse from under the counter.

"Save the romances for me to shelve," she pleaded. "I can't wait to see what you ordered."

"You got it. And, Karen…"

"Yes?"

"Thanks for sharing today with me."

"You're welcome. But I'm the one who should be thanking you for including me in this grand adventure."

That's exactly what it was, Andi thought as she dug into another carton. A grand adventure.

She'd gathered the statistics, knew that a third of all small businesses failed within three years. She also recognized that independent booksellers faced an uphill battle given the deep discounts and incentives publishers offered the big chains. Yet the thrill of being her own boss, of having complete control from start to finish over A Great Read, had brought her rolling out of bed every morning these past several weeks.

Okay, every morning but this one. She stared unseeing into the carton she'd just opened, remembering how she'd nestled in the crook of Dave's arm. Remembering as well the yeasty and achingly familiar scent of their lovemaking.

The muscles low in her belly tightened. She could almost feel Dave driving into her, his hips pumping, hers slamming upward in instinctive, primitive response.

She'd make her appearance at the town council *extremely* brief, Andi vowed.

SHOWERED AND CHANGED into linen slacks and a tropical-print blouse, Andi showed up at the Elks Hall a little before seven. The mayor spotted her immediately. Waving her forward, he sabotaged her plans to sit unobtrusively at the back of the hall and slip out early.

"Colonel Armstrong! Glad you could make it. Let me introduce you to the folks on the council."

As promised, Frost had shown Andi's videotape to the attorney kept on retainer by the town of Gulf Springs. He'd also discussed the situation with the council members. They were quick to thank Andi for exposing Talbot. They also agreed the tape might be challenged in a court of law but constituted sufficient grounds to terminate Bud Talbot's on-call contract as a building inspector.

Apparently word of the videotape had leaked beyond the council. As Al Frost introduced Andi to some of the other attendees, a number of them commented on it.

"He put the squeeze on me a few years back," the

operator of a charter fishing service admitted. "Said he'd have to recalculate the weight-stress standards for my pier. I had a six-man charter from Chicago flying in the next day. It was either slip Bud a fifty or move my boat and all my gear to another dock."

"He hit me up, too," the drugstore owner revealed. "Cost me a hundred before he approved the wiring for my new freezer unit."

With a look of exasperation on his liver-spotted face, the mayor challenged the two men. "Why didn't you boys tell me what Bud was up to?"

"Should have, I suppose." The boat captain pushed back his cap and scratched his head. "Guess I felt he was doin' me a favor by fudging his inspection report by a few pounds."

"Good thing the colonel here doesn't go in for those kinds of favors. By the way," Frost added slyly, "I've asked her to fill the empty seat on the council. I'm hoping y'all will help me persuade her."

The other men hopped right on that wagon, as did several members of the council, but Andi was too experienced at committee warfare to be roped in so easily. Smiling, she avoided making any commitments and settled in to watch the council in action.

Fifteen minutes into the meeting, she was mentally admonishing the mayor for not adhering to his published agenda. Discussion rambled from one topic to the next and back again several times before anyone thought to bring an issue to a vote. Anyone in the hall with something to say was allowed to speak, whether on topic or not.

Andi kept silent during the long-winded debate over an upgrade to the lighting at the public beach just east of town. She also refrained from comment after one of the council members suggested resurfacing the municipal parking lot but offered no solid financials to support the proposal.

She got sucked in, however, when the mayor introduced a proposal for a memorial to veterans to be erected in the small park at the end of Main Street.

"So many of our residents are serving or have served in the military," Frost said with a smile and a nod in Andi's direction. "We want to honor their service."

When he propped an artist's sketch up on the table, Andi leaned forward for a closer look. The design was really well done, a skillful blend of natural elements like crushed-shell walks and colorful oleanders. A circular granite wall depicted the dates of the country's major conflicts. Engraved on the wall were quotes from the great personages of each period. A static display of a Navy F-18 Hornet about to soar into flight dominated the center of the memorial.

"Tom Chester honchoed this project before he vacated his seat on the council and moved away," the mayor announced. "He'd talked to the Navy about acquiring an F-18 from the boneyard. From all reports, they weren't very helpful."

He'd addressed his remarks to the assembled group, but Andi knew darn well he was talking to her. Reluctantly she raised her hand.

"F-18s are still the mainstay of the Navy. They take a beating during catapult launches and the controlled crash known as a carrier landing. As a consequence, the Navy cannibalizes older F-18s in the boneyard for parts. It's doubtful they'll release one for static display until the airframe is stripped bare. You might want to consider another aircraft for the memorial."

"Which would you suggest?"

He'd reeled her in now. Andi acknowledged as much with a wry smile.

"As you well know, Hurlburt Field is the home of Special Operations Command Headquarters. Since it's right across the Inland Waterway, I'd go with a Special Ops airframe. Either a C-130 Hercules or one of their specially configured helos."

"She's right," the charter boat captain chimed in. "The folks at Hurlburt are our closest neighbors. We ought to be working with them on this memorial."

"I understand you have a connection to Hurlburt," the mayor said with bland understatement. "Think you could talk to him about our project?"

Andi planned to do a lot more than talk to her connection—when and if she ever got out of this meeting. In the interests of expediting matters, she nodded.

"I can do that."

"Maybe you could also take the artist's design specs and get some estimates as to labor and costs. Dan Gillmore here works at a Home Depot over in Pensacola. He'll help with the estimates."

"THAT'S ALL IT TOOK," Andi confessed as she and Dave walked along the beach sometime later. "One artist's sketch, a little unsubtle arm-twisting, and I find myself agreeing to fill an unexpired term on the Gulf Springs town council."

Pant legs rolled up, she splashed through the warm surf alongside Dave. He'd carried his beer with him. Although Doc Ramirez had given the green light concerning alcohol, Andi had opted for a bottle of unsweetened tea. Sue Ellen's champagne had gone straight to her head last night. She wanted to be completely sober for whatever happened tonight.

"I can see how a project like the memorial would snag your interest," Dave said, his deep baritone a counterpoint to the bubbling chatter of the surf. "You sure you have the time or the energy for it right now?"

"I don't see it taking too much of either. I worked out a preliminary action plan in my head and…"

"You don't have to tell me. You stopped at Wal-Mart on the way home, bought a three-ring binder and have already penciled tabs for each phase of the project."

"Hey, I'm not that anal."

His teeth showed in a quick, slashing grin. "Yeah, babe, you are."

"I didn't buy a binder," she informed him loftily.

"Because you already had one at the house?"

"Maybe."

"With tabs?"

"Maybe."

"And the different-colored clips you use to indicate action completed or still pending?"

Laughing, she came off her high horse. "All right, I like things neat and organized. So shoot me."

"How about I get you all messy and unorganized instead?"

She hooked a brow. "Think you can?"

"I know I can. Come here, woman."

Heat shooting from her neck to her knees, Andi went into his arms. She jumped out of them a half second later, screeching at the ice-cold jolt to her spine.

"Dammit, Armstrong. No fair using your beer can as a weapon."

"You know us Special Tactics types. We use whatever object's at hand to—oi!" It was his turn to bellow and jerk away from the stream of cold tea aimed at his midsection.

"*Oi?*" Smirking, Andi whipped the plastic bottle in a slashing arc and hit him with another spray. "What is that? Some new Special Ops term? What happened to manly grunts and hooh-ahs?"

"You want grunts? I'll give you grunts."

As wet now from the surf they kicked up as from tea and the brew spilling out of his can, he ducked under her firing arm and caught her by the middle.

"Dave! No!"

Ignoring her shrieks, he dragged her down with him. Sand and surf churned as they rolled over and over, each fighting for supremacy.

It wasn't much of a contest. Andi was no match for his strength. She thought about resorting to cunning but couldn't work up any real objections to the feel of his body pinning hers to the sand.

"Okay, okay," she huffed, soaked and out of breath. "I concede."

He knew her too well to accept such an easy victory. Eyes glinting in the light reflected from the iridescent sea-washed shore, he demanded clarification.

"Is this a surrender or merely a cease-fire to give you time to marshal your forces for a counterattack?"

A wave flattened against the shoals, foamed up the beach and washed over them. Sputtering, Andi spit out sandy saltwater.

"I surrender, you moron. Now let me up before we both drown."

"Not yet." Shifting his weight, Dave slid an arm under her shoulders to lift her above the outgoing eddies. "Are we talking complete and unconditional?"

She knew he was referring to more than this little skirmish. So much for his promise not to push, she thought wryly. And how like the man to choose this time and this place to make a stand.

Her hair floated around her head. What she sincerely hoped was a strand of slimy kelp was draped over her left ankle. Sand had worked its way inside her slacks *and* her panties. Yet Andi knew the frolic in the surf had propelled her into another decision.

She didn't want this moment to end. Ever. Or the cessation of hostilities.

Her breath sighing out, she went limp. Her hands came up to frame his face. She searched Dave's eyes, found what she was looking for and smiled.

"Complete and unconditional."

She got her grunt then. Marveling that such a small,

inarticulate sound could convey so much smug male triumph, she was ready when Dave swooped in for the coup de grâce.

As merciful deathblows went, this one was pretty damned effective. His mouth ground into hers. Teeth scraped. Tongues dueled for a moment or two before Andi locked her arms around his neck in total, glorious capitulation.

It took another wave to seal the terms of surrender. Crashing onto the shore, the seawater pounded into them and left Andi spitting out sand and salt again.

"For God's sake, Armstrong! Do you want to swim, surf or make love?"

"You need to ask?"

"Well, we can't do it here. I have something slimy draped over my ankle and I refuse to bare my butt to the sand crabs."

"As long as you bare it to me, I don't care where we do it."

"A bed, big guy. I want a bed. Soft sheets. Air-conditioning."

Rolling to his feet, Dave tugged Andi to hers.

"One bed, two sheets and thirty thousand BTUs of chilled air coming right up. Just don't plan on leaving them anytime in the near future."

CHAPTER 15

Looking back, Andi would always remember the last frantic days before her grand opening as the calm before the real storm hit.

She and Karen cut, opened, scanned and shelved like crazy women. When the shelf stock was arranged to their satisfaction, they tackled the front window.

They'd saved the boxes containing Roger Brent's latest hardback for the main display. Shaded by the glare-reducing window coating Andi had installed, they arranged *Return to Avaranche* into a towering, stair-stepping pyramid. Additional copies of the five-hundred-page thriller filled every available side shelf.

"That ought to catch a few folks' attention," Andi declared when she and Karen stepped back to view their handiwork. "Now for the banner."

With Karen's help, she unrolled the twelve-foot-long plastic-coated banner announcing the time and date of Roger Brent's appearance. Once they had hung it above and behind the pyramid, they went outside to survey the overall effect. A happy Karen brushed back strands of wildly curling red hair and pronounced judgment.

"That ought to catch *everyone's* eye."

Andi agreed. The windows done, she sat down to fire off follow-up press releases to run for three days before the big event.

The phone calls began the next day. So frequent were the requests to confirm Roger Brent's appearance that Andi recorded the time, location and general directions on the shop's answering machine.

In the midst of this whirl of last-minute preparations, she managed to snatch a few hours to work on the memorial project. Dave aided by tasking his exec to check into requirements for acquiring an aircraft from the boneyard at Davis-Monthan AFB outside Tucson.

Two days before the official grand opening, she and Karen divvied up the map to distribute flyers and posters. Their intent was to leave stacks at every shop, restaurant and library that would agree to hang or hand them out.

Sue Ellen and Crash helped by teaming up to cover Whiting Field and the Pensacola area. Before they drove off with a trunk full of fliers, S.E. provided a follow-on report to her earlier account of post-dining-out activities. Andi, in turn, admitted she now spent as many nights at Dave's place as he did at hers.

"Must be what accounts for your healthy glow," Sue Ellen teased. "Or did that spring from the doc's report?"

"Nothing like being declared bug-free to give a girl rosy cheeks."

Tapping a red-tipped nail against her chin, Sue Ellen looked her friend up and down.

"Nope," she declared after a moment. "It's the sex. Whatever other faults Dave Armstrong may possess, he could always ring your bell."

"Like Crash rings yours?"

"Man, does he ever! I bong like Big Ben striking midnight."

Choking, Andi shoved a stack of posters into her friend's arms. "You're shameless, woman."

"I try."

Smug as a pixie-faced Cheshire cat, S.E. glanced through the shop window to where Crash was loading boxes of flyers into his truck. When she pulled her gaze back, her expression turned serious.

"Level with me, Andi. Have you and Dave patched things up to the point where you might take your wedding rings out for a second run?"

"We're not quite there, but we're inching closer to it."

"I'm not sure how I feel about that. He hurt you, girl-friend. Bad."

"We hurt each other. If we do decide to go for a second run, we'll do things differently."

"I hope so."

Thankfully Sue Ellen left it at that. Andi had too much going on to provide a detailed analysis of what went wrong the first time around or exactly what they'd do differently this time.

The conversation stuck with her all day, however, and slipped into her mind again when she turned onto the cul-de-sac she shared with Dave late that evening. A quick glance at his house showed no lights.

A quick glance at *her* place had her stomping on the brake, her thoughts skidding to a stop along with the Tahoe. Even before the headlights picked out the Ohio license plate on the vehicle parked in her drive, she recognized her sister's much-dinged Dodge Caravan.

When Andi pulled into the driveway, Carol emerged from the minivan. The interior lights illuminated her thin, trembling frame and tear-ravaged face. Fear curdled Andi's stomach. An almost forgotten prayer ricocheted around in her head.

Please, God, please don't let it be drugs.

Carol had been clean for so many years. Hoping against hope she hadn't yielded to the insidious craving users said never left them, Andi jumped out of the Tahoe.

"What are you doing in Florida? Why didn't you call and let me know you were coming? What's going on?"

"I—I…"

Carol trembled so violently she couldn't speak. Sick with dread, Andi held out her arms. Her sister fell into them and burst into wrenching sobs.

Andi held her, just held her, until the sobs gave way to long, wracking shudders. When those subsided to gasping hiccups, she slid an arm around her sister's waist.

"Let's go into the house. We'll talk about it."

Whatever *it* was.

ACROSS THE INLAND Waterway, Dave was on his way out of the office and about to head home when his exec caught him.

"General Howard is on the line, sir."

Nodding, Dave retraced his steps. The Special Ops general serving as deputy commander of CENTCOM could be calling on any one of a half dozen hot issues.

Dave wasn't prepared for the one Howard hit him with, however.

"Your assignment as commander of Joint Task Force Six is back on, Armstrong. Pack your gear. You're going to Qatar."

Well, hell!

With his stomach nosing into a dive, Dave had to fight to keep his voice even.

"How did that happen? I thought the Navy wanted someone with a background in amphibious assault and had lobbied to put one of their own in command."

"It took some time and some doing, but I convinced CINCCENT to nix Navy's end run. JTF-6 is all yours, Dave. Congratulations."

"Yes, sir."

That was the best he could manage at the moment. Talk about your basic rotten timing! He'd been pissed when the Navy had blocked his assignment a few months back. Now he wished like hell they'd succeeded in placing a frog in command of the task force that would eventually include more than a thousand special forces from all branches of the service.

"This interservice wrangling has cost us," Howard said crisply. "You don't have much time to brief your deputy and turn over command of the 720th. I need you in Qatar by the end of next week."

Dave clicked instantly into prep mode. As he had so many times before, he began tabulating the tasks that needed doing before he hopped a transport. He got as far as the second task before his thoughts came to a dead stop.

He couldn't leave Andi. Not now. Not again.

His gaze shot to the framed photos on his office wall. The warrior in him reared up and bellowed a denial.

The hell he couldn't! His men needed him more than his ex-wife did right now. Doc Ramirez had just handed her a get-out-of-jail-free card. She'd be busy with the shop for weeks and months to come. Sue Ellen could keep an eye on her while Dave was in Qatar.

General Howard interrupted the fierce internal monologue. "I've laid on a briefing for you by the CENTCOM staff tomorrow afternoon. There are things we need to cover that can't be discussed over the phone. Plan to arrive by thirteen hundred."

"Yes, sir."

THE CALL PLAYED IN Dave's head repeatedly as he drove through the October night. Storm clouds had piled up over the gulf, obscuring the moon and pretty well matching his mood. His disposition didn't improve when he turned onto the cul-de-sac and spotted the Dodge Caravan parked in Andi's drive. One glimpse of the Ohio plates had him spitting out a curse.

Dammit all to hell! Just what he needed after General Howard's bombshell—an unannounced visit by Andi's sister and her smart-ass husband.

He was tempted to pull into his drive and leave them to Andi. Richard Perle had never been one of Dave's favorite people. His mild disdain for the smarmy divorce lawyer had morphed into outright dislike when Perle insisted on representing Andi.

Until that point, the divorce had been uncontested. In typical Andi fashion, she'd worked out every minute detail ahead of time. But Perle had still tried his damnedest to put the screws to his onetime brother-in-law.

Watching Perle's expression when Dave walked in and kissed Andi wouldn't provide near the satisfaction of planting a fist in the man's face, but he suspected Andi wouldn't appreciate blood gushing onto her carpet. Saving that anticipated pleasure for another time and place, Dave parked and walked across the driveways.

Andi met him at the door. "Carol's here."

"I saw the car." Dragging off his beret, he shoved it in the pocket of his BDUs. "Perle with her?"

"No. She drove down by herself. She just got here a few moments ago, so I don't have the full story yet, but apparently Richard's having an affair."

"I always said he was a slimy bastard."

"I know, I know." Distracted, she raked a hand through her hair and threw a glance over her shoulder. "Carol's a mess, Dave."

"Want me to come back later?"

She pursed her lips, thought about it and shook her head. "She likes you. Always has. She still says letting you walk out of my life was the worst mistake I ever made."

"She's got that right. Have you told her I'm muscling my way back in?"

"Not yet. As I said, she just got here a little while ago and, well, I don't think this is the right time to lay that on her."

Or lay General Howard's call on her sister, Dave thought grimly. The evening was producing one unwelcome surprise after another.

"Carol knows we're neighbors. I've told her we're on speaking terms again. Let's leave it at that for now."

Nodding, Dave followed her into the great room. He thought the reunion with his former sister-in-law might be awkward, but Carol welcomed him back into the fold with a watery smile.

"You were right, Dave. Richard's a pig."

"Did I call him a pig? Sure didn't mean to insult them that way."

Carol's smile held for another second or two before crumbling. The tissue in her hand shredded. Tears slid down her cheeks. Clicking her tongue, Andi dropped onto the sofa beside her and slid an arm around her.

With the two women huddled shoulder to shoulder, Dave folded his frame into an easy chair. Looking at them, he thought, you'd never guess they were sisters.

Carol's hair was the same dark mink as Andi's, her green eyes only a shade lighter, but the physical similarities ended there. Thin and pale and nervous, Carol looked as though *she* was the one infected with a penicillin-resistant bacterium.

As Dave knew all too well, the differences went more than skin-deep. Andi's core was solid steel. Her years as an officer had tempered that steel and imbued her with a quiet but unshakable self-confidence and the ability to take command of any situation.

Carol possessed that same strength—she couldn't have kicked her teenaged drug habit otherwise—but that experience had undermined her self-esteem and destroyed her confidence in herself. The fear that she would weaken and turn back to drugs never quite left her. Dave could hear echoes of it now in her quavering recital of infidelity and heartbreak.

"I'd suspected for some time," she said, her white-knuckled hand gripping Andi's. "Richard started working late or saying he had a meeting downtown or had stopped for a drink with the other attorneys on his way home."

Andi squeezed her sister's hand. "You suspected but you didn't say anything?"

"I was afraid to," Carol related miserably. "At first. Then I was, well, sort of relieved. Things have been rocky between us for such a long time. You know, like they were between you and Dave before you split."

Andi winced and left it to Dave to mutter a sardonic, "Yeah, we know."

"Then I saw them together," Carol continued. "Richard and his girlfriend. Last night. They were going into a restaurant. They had their arms around each other. They were laughing, happy."

More tears spilled down her pale cheeks.

"Richard and I haven't laughed in years. Really laughed. Seeing him like that, realizing how the joy had disappeared from our life, I...I kind of lost it."

"Lost it how?" Andi asked, her expression tight and anxious.

Dave guessed what she was thinking. His own thoughts were pretty grim. Hoping to hell Carol hadn't slipped back into the void, he set his jaw as the elder sister hung her head.

"I drove my car right up on the sidewalk," she confessed in a shaky voice. "Then I jumped out and whacked Richard with a bottle of Diet Pepsi."

Andi's mouth opened, shut and opened again. Relief, anxiety and incredulity all played across her face.

"Why, uh, Diet Pepsi?"

"I was on my way home from the grocery store. The Pepsi bottle was the closest weapon at hand." She lifted her head. A glimmer of satisfaction worked its way through her tears. "I knocked him flat on his ass."

"Good for you, sis!"

Dave echoed her sentiments. "Way to go, Carol."

She basked in their approval for a few moments before her triumph faded. Shoulders slumping, she gripped her sister's hand. "After I saw him hit the sidewalk, I got in my car and headed for the interstate. So here I am."

Andi's brows soared. "Whoa! Are you saying you didn't go home? Pack a suitcase? Clean out the bank account?"

"No. I wanted away from Richard as fast and as far as I could get. I didn't stop except to gas up the car en route. I thought—that is, I hoped—I could stay here with you until I figure out what to do next."

"Of course you can."

Andi's reply was swift and unhesitating, but the glance she sent Dave suggested she hadn't missed the irony of the situation. Nor had he.

Two sisters, both in transition. One with her marriage falling apart, the other in the process of patching hers back together.

Realizing that process had just hit a speed bump, Dave rose. "You must be exhausted after driving all that way. And hungry if you didn't stop for anything but gas. How about I scramble us up some eggs?"

"Thanks, but I couldn't eat anything." Carol gave a

ghost of a laugh. "I had five sacks of groceries in the car. I feasted on potato chips, seedless grapes and chocolate éclairs all the way down here."

"You may not want anything, but Andi needs to eat."

Chastened, the older sister turned a stricken face to the younger. "Oh, God, that's right. I've been so wrapped up in my own misery I didn't even ask you how you're doing."

"I'm okay."

"She needs to eat," Dave repeated, ignoring Andi's not-now frown. "I'll cook. Twenty minutes. My place."

Halfway to the door, he turned back to Carol. "I don't have any sympathy for Richard, but you've been gone for going on twenty-four hours now."

"He won't care."

"Maybe not, but you should call him, let him know you're okay so he doesn't have the police out looking for you."

"I don't want to talk to him now. Maybe not ever."

"Want me to make the call?"

"Would you?"

He showed his teeth. "With pleasure."

IT WAS CLOSE TO MIDNIGHT by the time Andi got her sister settled in the guest room. By then, Carol had talked herself hoarse.

The hurt, the disgust, the self-pity had all spilled out, accompanied by more tears and, toward the end, a healthy bout of anger. Her hands had shaken and her whole body had trembled at one point, but to Andi's profound relief, not once had her sister voiced a desperate desire for a hit.

"She's beaten it," Andi reported to Sue Ellen in a quick call the next morning. "She's really beaten it."

"I hope so."

"I know so, S.E." Wedging the phone under her ear, Andi poured two glasses of orange juice. "You and I have both been through the breakup of a marriage. You know how it rips you apart. She had the strength to come here instead of staying in Ohio and wallowing in her misery."

"How's she going to handle the fact that you and Dave are getting back together just when her own marriage is falling apart?"

"She'll handle it."

Andi infused her reply with more confidence than she actually felt. Carol liked Dave. She always had. Still, Andi didn't want to rub the wonder and excitement and lust she and Dave had regenerated in her sister's face.

Then there was the bookstore. How would her sister react to the project that had injected such excitement and fun into Andi's life?

Carol loved books almost as much as she did. Their

father's military career and frequent moves had prompted both sisters to turn to fictional friends after leaving yet another school and set of playmates. Wisely their mom had stocked up on Nancy Drew, Girl Detective novels and Tamora Pierce's Immortals adventures before bundling the family into the car for another cross-country drive.

Still, seeing the newness of Andi's store, the thrill it gave her, might only emphasize the empty hole looming in Carol's life. Unfortunately that was a chance Andi had to take. With her grand opening just over twenty-four hours away, she couldn't stay home and commiserate with her sister. Instead she'd offered to put her to work.

"Sorry to cut this short, but I've got to roust Carol out of bed. She's going into the shop with me today. She said she wants to keep busy while she decides what she's going to do next."

"You two are definitely sisters. Me? I'd fly down to Cabo San Lucas and spend a week at a spa."

"Being oiled and pummeled by a hunky young masseur?"

"Of course. Why else would anyone go to a spa?"

Snorting, Andi returned the juice carton to the fridge and issued a quick invitation. "Dave said he had to drive over to CENTCOM headquarters this afternoon and won't be back until late. Why don't you join Carol and me for dinner? I'll ask Karen if she can join us, too."

"Sounds good to me. I'll swing by the shop after work."

"See you then."

CHAPTER 16

"**It's** just a small shop," Andi warned as she steered the Tahoe down Gulf Springs's main street. "Nothing like the Town-and-Country bookstore in Dayton."

Her sister shrugged aside the comparison. "That store is so huge you can get lost in it."

"I tailored my selections to my target customer base. You won't find the same variety as in a big chain."

"I wouldn't expect to."

Ridiculously nervous about showing off her baby, Andi spotted a headful of bright red hair in the vehicle just ahead.

"That's Karen Duchek. She's my only employee at this point. She's as addicted to books as I am. Correction—as addicted as *we* are."

Smiling, Carol delved into their bank of shared memories. "Remember the summer we discovered Georgette Heyer?"

"How could I forget? You got your license that summer. Dad went ballistic at all the miles we put on the car, driving from library to library."

Those were the long-ago days before Internet book-stores…and before either sister could afford to buy books instead of borrowing them from a public library.

"It took us most of the summer," Andi recalled, "but we managed to track down every Georgette Heyer in a three-state region."

"Then we'd take our latest finds to that Italian place on Route 7 and hog a booth for hours, scarfing down spa-ghetti and pizza and garlic bread while we read. *Friday's Child* is still my all-time favorite."

It would be, Andi thought on a rush of affection. Like the timid heroine in that book, Carol had discovered a core of strength she hadn't realized she possessed and conquered personal demons.

"I love *The Grand Sophy*. I reread it every few years."

"Why am I not surprised?" Pretending to be deep in thought, Carol drummed her fingers on the leather armrest. "How did the other characters in the book describe Sophy? I think the term was *managing*."

"Hey, some folks are managing and some are just well organized. I happen to fall into the latter category."

Her sister huffed in derision. "*Well organized* doesn't come close to describing you, my child. Do you still in-ventory and color code your CDs?"

"Of course. What else are color tabs and spreadsheets for? Speaking of which…"

Pulling into the parking slot next to Karen, Andi killed the Tahoe's engine and grabbed her tote from the backseat.

"Wait until you see the inventory scanning-and-ordering system we've set up. It's *mucho* slick."

Carol didn't answer. Andi turned to find her staring openmouthed at the window display.

"Roger Brent?" she gasped. "Here? Tomorrow?"

Andi swallowed a sigh of relief. Judging by Carol's reaction, she'd derive as much pleasure from the shop as her sister did.

"In the flesh," she answered happily.

"Omigod. I *loved Blood Squad*."

"Wait until you read *Return to Aravanche*. It's even better."

Descending from the Tahoe, Andi hailed her employee. "Hey, Karen. This is my sister, Carol. She's a hopeless bibliophile, too."

Looking more like a teenager than a mother in her flower-print smock dress and round-toed Mary Janes, Karen smiled a welcome. "Nice to meet you. Andi didn't mention you were coming down to Florida for her grand opening."

"She didn't know."

"It was a spur-of-the-moment decision," Andi said, smoothly deflecting any further explanations until Carol felt ready to give them. "Come on, sis. Karen and I will give you the two-dollar tour. Then we all roll up our sleeves and prepare for the hordes that will descend on us tomorrow."

Praying her breezy prediction proved true, she unlocked the door, deactivated the alarm and ushered her sister and her employee into the world of mystery, adventure and romance.

THE THREE WOMEN WORKED nonstop the entire day. Andi spent most of it doing phone interviews with local radio stations eager to follow up on the PR Brent's publisher had sent out. Carol got busy unboxing and scanning the additional copies of *Return to Avaranche* ordered in at the last minute.

Karen was in charge of refreshments. After checking with Heather and Sam across the street to make sure they'd deliver the promised platters of boiled shrimp, buffalo wings and fried mozzarella sticks, she hit the bakery. There she confirmed their order for cookies and the monster cake decorated with the shop's logo. That done, she picked up cups, plates and napkins from the Hallmark store farther down Main and the colorful pennants Andi wanted to string from street lamp to street lamp.

"Are you sure it's okay to put these up?" Carol asked,

looping a strand over one shoulder. "Don't you need permission from the city or something?"

"I am the city," Andi confessed. "You're looking at a member of the town council."

"You're kidding! How did that happen?"

"Same way the bookshop happened. Seems I have this constitutional need for perpetual motion. And, yes, I duly submitted my request in writing and received permission from the mayor himself. Wait here. I'll get the ladder."

Remembering the near catastrophe the last time she'd climbed up and overextended, Andi positioned the ladder carefully. She was about to mount it when Sue Ellen drove up with Crash.

Carol knew S.E. from previous visits to her sister. This was her first exposure to Major Bill Steadman, however. Karen's, as well.

The two women managed to refrain from ogling—barely!—but even Andi gulped when the curly-haired Adonis swung out of S.E.'s low-slung sports car.

"We thought you might need some last-minute muscle," Sue Ellen announced, gliding a proprietary palm over Crash's biceps. "We're here to serve."

"I'll take that," he said, reaching for the ladder.

With Crash to do the hanging, Andi formed a chain with Karen and Carol to feed him the pennants while Sue Ellen eyeballed his placement. Their activities brought out other shop owners and interested bystanders. Several lent willing hands.

In the midst of the activity, Karen's husband and boys arrived on the scene. The boys' hair was as coppery red as their mother's, their spirits every bit as lively as she'd warned.

"This is Ben." Beaming with pride, Karen tapped two bright heads in turn. "This is Charlie. And this is my husband, Jerry."

Still in uniform, Staff Sergeant Duchek offered Andi a handshake and a warm smile. "Karen's talked nonstop about this shop since the day she started here. She's thrilled to be part of it."

"Not as thrilled as I am to have her."

"We brought the video games for the kids' section," Ben announced, clutching a plastic sack. "They're really cool."

"Thanks for picking them out for me. Want to test them on the computer while we finish here?"

"Sure."

The boys darted for the door. Their mom hastily followed. "I'd better supervise. Jerry, will you help here?"

With so much assistance, stringing the remaining pennants went fast. Soon eye-popping neon flags crisscrossed Main Street for an entire block before arrowing toward the front door of A Great Read.

"Looks good," Sue Ellen observed, dusting her hands on the seat of her designer jeans. "Very good, if I do say so myself. What's the next item on your checklist?"

"There isn't one. We're done."

Her pansy eyes widened in astonishment. "I don't believe it. You've actually run out of to dos?"

"For tonight. No, wait. There is one more item."

"I knew it."

"Dinner. My treat." Her happy grin encompassed Sue Ellen, Crash, Carol and the Ducheks. "We'll make it our very own prelaunch party."

In short order they had the boxes compacted, the computers shut down, the ladder put away and the shop locked. Feeling like a general at the head of a column, Andi led her troops across the street to Cap'n Sam's.

Heather seated them at a round table near the window. Sam tipped his spatula in greeting and promised to fry up a fresh batch of hush puppies. The boys kept things so lively and the laughter flowed so freely that Andi almost missed her cell phone's ringtone.

Her pulse sped up when she glanced at caller ID and saw Dave's name on the screen. He was all she needed to make the celebration complete. To make her *family* complete, she amended with a flutter of quiet joy.

"Where are you?" she asked by way of greeting.

"On my way back from MacDill. Where are you?"

"At Cap'n Sam's."

"Sounds like half of Gulf Springs is there with you."

"Nope, just Carol, Sue Ellen, Crash, Karen, her husband, Jerry, and her boys. We're having a preopening celebration. Come join us."

"I will, but I'm at least a half hour out."

"No problem. We just put our order in. We'll still be chowing down when you get here."

"Okay."

He added something else, but the background noise drowned him out.

"What did you say?"

"I said I need to talk to you. Maybe we could walk down to the beach after we get home."

"Sure." She turned a shoulder to the others and lowered her voice to a husky promise. "Or we could go back to your place for a private party."

"Private sounds good. See you shortly."

"That was Dave," Andi announced to the group. "He's going to join us, but it might be a while. He's on his way back from CENTCOM headquarters."

Crash looked up from the tic-tac-toe game he and Ben had sketched on the paper place mat.

"Did he say whether he got the assignment?"

Andi's happy grin slipped. Carefully she laid her cell phone beside her paper-wrapped plastic knife and fork.

"What assignment?"

Crash grimaced and looked as though he'd just swallowed a particularly vile oath. "Sorry," he muttered. "I shouldn't have said anything. It's still just a rumor."

"*What* is?"

"JTF-6. The rumors are flying at Whiting Field that Colonel Armstrong will get command."

Frowning, Sue Ellen jumped in. As a former military spouse, she knew what the initials stood for in general but not the specific designation. "What and where is JTF-6?"

"A multiservice Special Ops task force," Andi replied, struggling for breath. "Headquartered at Al-Udeid Air Base in Qatar."

"Dave's going to the Persian Gulf? Sh—" S.E. glanced at the boys, caught herself just in time and finished with a lame, "Shoot!"

Karen and her husband exchanged quick glances. Crash squirmed in his chair. Carol chewed on her lower lip, obviously trying to assess the impact of Dave's assignment on her sister.

Andi could have told her. She felt as though a big, black chasm had just opened up under her feet. Her throat tight, she quizzed Crash.

"I thought—that is, Dave told me his assignment was canceled."

"It was. The Navy lobbied all the way to the president

to put one of their own in that billet. Poindexter supposedly had it in the bag, but, well…"

He glanced around the table, seeking help. All he got was a fierce scowl from Sue Ellen, frowns from the other adults and puzzled looks from the boys. Blowing out a breath, Crash tried to ease the blow.

"JTF-6 is a star maker. You watch, Andi. Dave will come out on the next general's list."

She stretched her lips until they cracked. "I hope so. He certainly deserves it. Oh, good. Here's Heather with our salads and hush puppies."

Dipping her chin, she pretended to fiddle with her utensils. She couldn't breathe, could barely think.

They'd come so close, she and Dave.

So *freaking* close!

Burying her hands in her lap, she wadded her paper napkin into a tight ball. She'd thought they'd get in at least six months or a year before they had to say goodbye again. Had hoped against hope they could fill the empty void of the past four years with bright new memories before they had to draw on them to get through another separation.

Dammit, they were going to do it right this time. Meld their lives, their work, their needs.

She wanted to weep with disappointment and frustration and the aching fear that she and Dave would lose each other a second time. Instead she faced a ring of worried friends and reached deep inside herself for a smile.

"Hey! This is supposed to be a celebration. Lift your glasses, everyone. We need a toast."

"I've got one." Sue Ellen thrust out her glass toward the center of the table. "Here's to A Great Read. May she reap many readers and much profit."

Beer and cola sloshed as seven other glasses clinked against hers.

"Hear, hear!"

"To A Great Read."

"To great sales."

Everyone got into the act after that, offering salutes to much-loved books, to bestselling authors in general and Roger Brent in particular, to favorite video games.

"Now me." Shy but determined, Karen shoved back her chair and rose. "Here's to you, boss. May all your dreams for yourself and your shop—"

"Our shop."

Her cheeks flushed with pleasure and pride. "May all your dreams for yourself and *our* shop come true."

Giving her best imitation of a woman whose dreams hadn't suddenly turned to salt, Andi raised her glass again.

"Thanks, Karen."

EVERYONE AT THE TABLE worked to maintain a gay atmosphere through the meal that followed. Andi stayed as animated as the others, but her mind kept zinging back to the possibility Dave had been tapped for command of the task force slated to go into Qatar.

Andi had been to Qatar, had witnessed some of the massive buildup of bases there in anticipation of the pullout from Iraq. She knew those bases would provide launch platforms for the highly skilled, highly mobile forces of JTF-6 in the event they had to make a lightning redeployment into Iraq or Iran or any other country that threatened the area's shaky stability.

She also knew the U.S. military weren't the only Americans in Qatar. One of her coworkers at the Pentagon had retired a few months before she did and was now a defense contractor pulling in big bucks. She could e-mail him, find out who she needed to talk to, see what openings the company had.

Gulping, she raised a hand and fingered the small, hard ridge on her chin. The prospect of going back to the biting desert winds and stinging sand made her feel sick. Almost as sick as the idea of closing her bookstore mere weeks or months after it opened.

Slowly she shifted in her seat until she had a clear view through the window. The strings of bright neon triangles glowed in the slowly gathering dusk. The timer on her shop sign had kicked on, illuminating the display beneath. The towering pyramid of *Return to Avaranche* made her chest squeeze.

They were just books, she reminded herself fiercely. Just words. They gave pleasure but not love. Hope but not commitment.

Her thoughts whirling, she stared at the shop across the street until a pair of headlights stabbed through the purple haze. Dave's pickup turned onto Main a second later.

Like iron filings dropped near a magnet, everything snapped into place. Andi's doubts fled and her decision came fast and sure.

Separate careers and separate assignments had driven a wedge between Dave and her once before. She would *not* let that happen again.

No more goodbyes, she vowed, shoving back her chair. No more empty nights. Whither thou goest, Armstrong, I'm damn well going, too.

"'Scuse me, folks. I need to talk to my husband."

Darting across the street, she waved Dave into the parking slot next to her Tahoe. He got out of his vehicle looking big and handsome and tough as hell in his boots, bloused BDUs and beret.

"I thought the party was at Cap'n Sam's," he commented as she rooted around in her purse for her shop keys.

"It was. Is. Everyone's still there, but we need to have that talk you mentioned. I thought it would be better if we had it here."

He didn't comment on the fact that the discussion they'd agreed to have later that night had suddenly moved up on the agenda. That told Andi he was as anxious to get it over with as she was. Jamming the key into the lock, she decided to make it easy on him.

"I know about the JTF-6 assignment, Dave."

"Well, hell! The word's already on the street?"

"It is."

She shouldered open the door, felt for the light switch and flicked it upward. The papery smell of books greeted her like an old friend and started her thoughts whirling. The lease on the store ran for six months. Depending on when Dave had to leave, maybe she could operate her shop for a while, see how it did, then either shut down or leave someone else in charge. Karen, if she could extend her hours. Or Carol, if she decided to stay in Florida.

Consumed by her thoughts, Andi was two or three steps into the store when she realized only the display spots had come on. The main fluorescent overheads remained dark. So, she noticed belatedly, did the alarm panel.

"What…?"

That's all she got out before she heard a faint whoosh coming from above her head. She craned her neck, searching the dimly lit ceiling. The next instant, water spewed from the sprinkler heads and sprayed downward, hitting Andi smack in the face.

She screeched.

Dave spit out a curse.

Then they both spun toward the sound of a crash as someone or something slammed into the panic bar on the back door.

CHAPTER 17

Dave sprinted through the pulsing spray, his boots like thunder on the now-slick floor as he pounded between two rows of shelves.

Andi was a half step behind him. Water rained down, drenching her hair, her clothes. She barely registered its sting. Her focus—her *only* focus—was Dave's broad-shouldered bulk.

In the two- or three-second time warp between hearing the sprinklers whoosh on, getting hit in the face and spinning toward the slam of the back door, one grim thought had penetrated the chaos inside her head: someone had been in the shop when she'd unexpectedly returned.

Now that her shocked mind had jolted back into gear, Andi had a damned good idea who that someone was. As she raced behind Dave, his earlier warning screamed inside her head.

You corner a junkyard dog, he'll go for your throat.

When Dave hit the panic bar on the back door and crashed into the alley behind the shop, Andi barreled through right behind him. He whirled left. She spun to the right and spotted a dim shadow flying down the alley toward a panel truck parked at the far end.

"There!"

She took off on a burst of speed fueled by pure unadulterated fury. It didn't enter her head that her prey might be armed or that she'd make an easy target in her light-colored blouse.

Both had evidently occurred to Dave. He overtook her halfway down the alley and locked on to her arm. Snarling, he swung her bodily toward a Dempsey Dumpster.

"You're too visible! Stay the hell out of his line of fire."

By contrast, his camouflage BDUs made him damn near *in*visible. He shot past Andi and was immediately swallowed by the darkness.

Scrunching her nose at the stink emanating from the Dumpster, she darted around the metal container and kept to the shadows as she panted after him. Suddenly a bull-like bellow shattered the night.

"Talbot!"

The man who'd wrenched open door of the panel truck jumped a good foot in the air. Whirling, he spotted what must have looked like a dim mountain charging straight at him. Cursing, he leaped into the driver's seat.

That was as far as he got. Dave was on him a second later, blocking his attempt to slam the door, dodging the boot aimed at his groin, hauling him out by the scruff of his neck.

Desperation made up for the fifty- or sixty-pound difference between the two men. Dave got in the first blow. Talbot swayed but somehow managed to stay on his feet. When he jerked his arm back, Andi saw what he had in his hand.

"Dave! He's got a wrench!"

He threw up an arm to block the blow, but Talbot got in under his guard. Bone crunched. Blood spurted. Grunting, Dave staggered back.

Andi didn't stop to think, didn't so much as blink. Shrieking with rage, she launched herself through the air.

"You bastard!"

No lightweight, she plowed into Talbot and slammed him to the ground. He hit hard, cracking his head against the pavement. One moan and he went out.

Andi didn't bother to check his pulse, didn't worry whether he was concussed, didn't care if he came to in the next instant and took off running. Jumping up, she whirled and almost let out another screech.

Dave loomed right behind her, blood gushing from his nose. His eyes were savage, his fists bunched. Dragging his gaze from the building inspector, he raked Andi with a hard glance. Apparently assured she was okay, he relaxed his predatory stance.

"Nice takedown, Armstrong."

She made a hiccuping sound that was halfway between a sob and a laugh. "Thanks."

The blood terrified her. The glistening red stream poured from his shattered nose. Andi threw a frantic glance around the dark alley, found nothing she could use and ripped off her blouse.

"Sit down," she ordered tersely, wadding the material into a ball. "Put your head back."

She got him positioned against one of the truck's wheels and put the wadded cloth in his hand. She didn't dare press it against his face herself.

"Do you have your cell phone?"

"In my shirt," he muttered through the cotton. "Right breast pocket."

THE GULF SPRINGS POLICE responded to Andi's call with gratifying speed. Siren screaming, lights flashing, the patrol car screeched to a halt at the end of the alley.

Andi recognized the uniformed officer who cut the siren and heaved himself out of the front seat. She'd met him on her first visit to the town offices. Hitching his gun belt over the mound of his stomach, the officer surveyed the man just starting to twitch back to consciousness.

"Yep, that's Bud Talbot. You say he broke in to your shop?"

On her knees beside Dave, Andi frowned. "We didn't actually see him inside. But we heard the back door slam, raced outside and saw him running down the alley."

"I yelled at him to stop." Dave kept his head tilted at a forty-five-degree angle. "Dragged him out of his truck. Bastard let swing with a wrench."

A loud moan drew their attention back to the building inspector. Woozy and obviously still half out of it, Talbot levered onto an elbow.

"Wh-what happened?"

"The colonel here decked you."

"Not me," Dave corrected drily. "The other colonel."

"You don't say."

Beaming his approval, the officer hooked a hand under Talbot's arm and dragged him to his feet.

"Come on, Bud. It'll take our volunteer firemen and EMT crew another ten, fifteen minutes to scramble. I'll drive you to the hospital, have your head X-rayed. Ms. Armstrong, you want to drive your husband? I have a poncho in the trunk you can pull on."

Andi had forgotten she'd sacrificed her blouse to Dave's bloody nose. Tugging the plastic poncho over her head, she was bending to assist Dave when a small herd charged around the corner.

Crash was in the lead, followed by Sergeant Duchek, Sue Ellen, Karen, Carol, Heather and what looked like most of the patrons from Cap'n Sam's. The boys were the only ones missing that Andi could tell. The crowd skidded to a collective halt and left Crash to rush the last few yards.

"We heard the siren," he bit out, offering Dave a strong hand to help him up. "Saw the patrol car cut around the block. Took us a minute to realize your shop lights hadn't come on and make the connection. Sorry."

"No problem." The blood-soaked rag muffled Dave's nonchalant reply. "Andi took care of the problem."

Part of the problem, she realized when Crash asked if she had the keys the Tahoe. "They're in my purse. In the shop." A groan ripped from the back of her throat. "Probably under a foot of water by now."

"What?"

"The sprinklers. Talbot turned them on."

"Oh, no!"

The shriek came from Karen. Sue Ellen and Carol added their dismay to hers.

"Your books!"

"They'll be soaked."

"Will someone please figure out how to turn the damn things off?" Andi pleaded. "Dave, you have your keys? We can take your pickup."

"I'm okay," he insisted. "You stay."

"Forget it, Armstrong. Whither thou goest…"

"Come again?"

"I'll explain later."

He let the explanation slide only until she had him in the backseat of his extended-cab pickup. Heather had dashed across to the restaurant and returned with ice wrapped in a towel, which Dave now held to what he insisted was only a broken nose. While Crash wheeled through the night with Sue Ellen strapped in beside him, Andi's wounded warrior pressed for details.

"What's this *whither* business?"

Gently she dabbed at the dried blood now crusting his chin and cheeks with a corner of the towel. "I did some hard, fast thinking after I heard about the JTF assignment. I'm going to Qatar with you."

The calm announcement whipped Sue Ellen's head around and earned a quick look in the rearview mirror from Crash. Dave gaped at her in startled silence above his ice pack.

"A friend of mine from the Pentagon is there now," Andi said, plunging ahead, "working as a civilian contractor. He can get me on. I'm sure I have some skills that would prove useful."

"You have a whole bagful, but…"

"No buts, Dave, and no more goodbyes. You said it yourself. We have to blend, become one."

Silence invaded the cab, broken only by the engine's

muted hum and the squeak of Sue Ellen's seat as she wiggled around for a better view.

"Yeah," Dave finally agreed, lowering the ice pack, "that's what I said."

"Then it's settled. Good thing I didn't put my boots and desert gear in storage."

"You won't need desert gear, Andi."

"Sure I will." She swiped gently at another streak of red. "I've been to Qatar. I know how hot and—"

"You won't need it." Reaching up, he caught her hand. "Neither will I. I turned down command of JTF-6."

"You—you couldn't," she stuttered. "You didn't."

"I could and I did."

She grasped the implications immediately. A drastic move like that would deep-six any chance at promotion and kill Dave's career. Senior officers didn't turn down assignments unless they were prepared to hang up their uniforms.

"But CENTCOM... General Howard..."

"I had to drive over there this afternoon. I figured I should tell the general face-to-face."

"But—but—"

He tried a grin, winced and settled for cupping her cheek. "No buts and not one more goodbye."

Thrown completely for a loop, she could only stare at his battered, gore-streaked face.

THEIR SECOND TRIP TO the ER in as many months took
several hours. The docs ordered a CT scan to make
sure the wrench hadn't caused any facial fractures
besides a dented nose. By the time the results came
back, Dave's nose had swollen to a bruised mound,
and the whites of his eyes glowed as red as the fires of
hell. Hiding a grin, the ER physician followed his
patient's terse instructions for proper placement of the
bandage.

"Taken a few blows to the face, Colonel?"

"One or two." Dave inspected the handiwork and
nodded. "Thanks, Doc, I'm good to go."

Crash and Sue Ellen were in the waiting room.

"Sergeant Duchek called a little while ago," S.E.
reported. "He had to take the boys home but said his wife
and your sister are still at the store."

"Did they get the sprinklers turned off?"

"Yes."

Sue Ellen's grim expression answered Andi's next
question before she asked it. "I take it the damage is
pretty bad."

"Yes again."

DESPITE THE ADVANCE warning, Andi held her breath
when she reentered the shop.

Carol and Karen stilled the mops they were wielding.

After making sympathetic noises over Dave's werewolf eyes and bandaged face, they both came close to tears as they watched Andi survey the ruin of her bright, shiny dream.

Her ficus drooped pathetically, its branches bent from its dousing. The paperbacks Andi had so lovingly unboxed, scanned and shelved now lay in sodden heaps on the floor. Every copy of *Return to Avaranche* stacked on the center round in preparation for Roger Brent's visit sported soaked, warped covers. Her beautiful window display floated in a foot of water.

Gulping down the golf ball that seemed to have lodged in her throat, Andi forced herself to think.

"I'll, uh, need to print a copy of our inventory for the insurance company."

"We tried the shop computer," Karen said miserably. "It's shorted out. So are the terminals."

"Good thing I backed up everything up on my laptop."

Her gaze went to the plastic-coated banner hanging above the remains of her pyramid. The four-foot letters defiantly announced Roger Brent's visit. Sighing, she added another item to her checklist.

"I've got Brent's phone number in my home computer, too. I'll contact him first thing in the morning to let him know the signing's canceled."

Talk about bad PR. Not only did she have to scrub the

bestselling author, she wouldn't be able to spread word of the cancellation in time to notify folks hoping for an autographed copy of his latest thriller. She doubted any of the disgruntled potential customers would return when—if—the shop ever reopened.

"Why cancel?"

Dave's question pulled her from what threatened to become a world-class funk.

"Huh?"

"Why cancel Brent's appearance."

"Kind of hard to host a book signing with no books."

"You ordered your stock from a distribution center in Tennessee, right?"

"Right."

"So order more. They operate a twenty-four-hour hotline, don't they?"

Andi quashed a sudden surge of hope. "They do, but even with expedited processing I could never get an order delivered in time. The distribution center is a good eight hours away."

"Not by air."

Hope leaped again, wild and joyful, as Dave turned to Crash.

"Are you certified on a civilian version of the Huey?"

"I'm current on C, D and F models."

"I'll make a quick call, wake a friend and we're on our way."

"Dave, no!" Andi's protest was instant and instinctive. "You can't fly all bunged up."

"I've done it before."

She couldn't let him take the risk. Not for a few books.

"If you hit altitude, you'll start bleeding again."

"We'll skim the treetops."

"It's not worth it, Dave. I can fall back, regroup, schedule another grand opening."

"And lose the impact of the publicity you've generated for this one."

"So I lose it."

"Sure you want to do that, Andi? You're not alone in this enterprise."

His gesture encompassed Karen, Sue Ellen, Carol, Crash.

"They've got a stake in the store. So do I."

"You? How?"

His red eyes gleamed fiendishly above the bandage taped over his nose. "I'm going to be out of a job soon, don't forget. I'm hoping I can talk you into taking me on as a partner. I figure the shop can support us both in the lifestyle we'd like to become accustomed to."

"Oh, right! I can see you behind the counter of a bookstore."

"Stranger things have happened. Get on the horn, woman. Put in your order and tell the distribution center we'll be there by first light to pick it up."

AGAINST ALL ODDS, ANDI and her crew of determined helpers pulled off one helluva event.

With the shop still soggy and uninhabitable, Andi had to find an alternate location. She considered, then decided against a sidewalk event. The sun would be too hot, the crowds too big. Thinking fast, she made a call to the mayor and got permission to move the book signing to the small park at the end of Main Street. She also called a local church to secure the loan of eight-foot folding tables.

Her crew reconvened at six the next morning. Jerry Duchek picked up and delivered the tables. While Andi and the boys set them up, Jerry went to work restringing neon pennants and hanging the plastic banner to mark the book signing's new locale.

Carol stayed at the shop to direct traffic to the new location. Sue Ellen and Karen ferried food, drinks and cartons of sales slips. Without her computerized system, Andi could only take cash, checks or, in a pinch, IOUs from the troops already starting to show. Since it was Saturday morning, most of them wore jeans and T-shirts, but there was no mistaking their buzz cuts. Sprinkled among them were a goodly number of women and civilians.

Andi and her assistants worked the crowd, passing out punch and the assortment of goodies Karen had picked up at the bakery. Roger Brent arrived right on schedule. With his shaved head and cobra tattoo snaking up one forearm, he lived up to his tough-guy image on the soaked copies of *Return to Avaranche*.

The long line already formed puffed up the author's chest. The empty tables lowered his brows.

"No books?" he asked after Andi had introduced herself, Sue Ellen and Karen.

"Not yet. They're on their way."

Or so the call she'd received from Dave several hours ago had assured her. They'd had the cartons loaded and had been about to lift off.

Signaling to Joe Goodwin, she detached him from a cluster of men and drew him to Brent's attention.

"You remember Chief Goodwin, don't you?"

"Sure do. How's that training camp for troubled teens coming, Joe?"

"Slowly," the chief replied with a sardonic glance at Sue Ellen. "But I'm hoping to cut through the red tape and open next summer."

"Let me know when you're up and running. I'd like to come out and take a look-see."

"Will do."

Desperate to kill a little more time, Andi suggested

the chief introduce the author to some of his troops. "He might get another book out of them."

Or not.

The chief made only a single introduction before Dave's pickup wheeled around the corner. Boxes were stacked four or five high in the truck bed. When Dave climbed out, still in his bandage and blood-soaked BDUs, Joe let loose with a long whistle.

"Hell, Colonel. What country did you just invade?"

"Tennessee."

Shooting Andi a wide grin, he moved to the back of the truck. "Major Steadman and I could use some help unloading these boxes."

"All right, troops. You heard the colonel. Fall in."

One year later

"I knew you wouldn't last behind the counter of a bookstore."

Smiling at her husband, Andi stacked chicken popovers in a straw basket. They'd decided against a dinner party to celebrate their first reanniversary but wanted to share their happiness with friends and family. Hence the picnic about to take place at the Gulf Springs Veterans Park against a backdrop of the H-130 Hercules recently mounted on a gleaming marble pedestal.

Andi couldn't think of any spot more fitting for their celebration. They were both veterans, proud of their service, happy in the life that had come after.

Dave underscored that new life when he curled a knuckle under Andi's chin and tipped her face to his.

"You didn't last very long behind the counter, either, Madam Mayor."

That was true! Andi still wasn't quite sure how i

had happened, but two months ago she'd made another right oblique and marched off in a direction she'd never anticipated.

"One term on the town council and the outgoing mayor talks me into running," she muttered. "I can't believe the fool citizens of Gulf Springs elected me."

"The citizens of Gulf Springs know a good thing when they see it. So do I. You won my vote, Armstrong."

"Thanks. I think."

Her duties didn't consume that much of her time. She still put in several hours a day at A Great Read. But Carol had taken over most of the daily operation, ably assisted by Karen.

To Andi's relief, her sister had expressed only heartfelt joy that she and Dave had found each other again while Carol herself pressed ahead with a divorce. The shop had become her haven, just as it had Andi's.

Dave, however, had found his own niche. As soon as word of his pending retirement leaked, Lockheed Martin asked him to head their Air Operations Center at Hurlburt.

Andi hadn't been surprised by the offer. The giant aerospace contractor was lucky as hell to get someone with his qualifications. The salary, however, had made her eyes pop.

Best of all, Dave traveled rarely and then only in short bursts. Most of the time he was home.

"Are you sure you're happy flying a desk?"

"I'm happy flying anything, Armstrong, as long as we do it in formation."

She searched his eyes, seeing the love, feeling the joy, and stretched up on tiptoe to brush her mouth over his.

"Me, too, Armstrong."

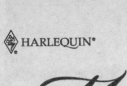

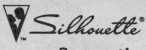

Silhouette®

Romantic
SUSPENSE

**Sparked by Danger,
Fueled by Passion.**

*This month and every month look for
four new heart-racing romances
set against a backdrop of suspense!*

Available in May 2007

Safety in Numbers
(Wild West Bodyguards miniseries)
by Carla Cassidy

Jackson's Woman
by Maggie Price

Shadow Warrior
(Night Guardians miniseries)
by Linda Conrad

One Cool Lawman
by Diane Pershing

Available wherever you buy books!

SRS0407

nocturne™

IT'S TIME TO DISCOVER THE RAINTREE TRILOGY...

There have always been those among us
who are more than human...

Don't miss the dramatic first book by
New York Times bestselling author

LINDA HOWARD

RAINTREE: *Inferno*

On sale May.

Raintree: Haunted by Linda Winstead Jones
Available June.

Raintree: Sanctuary by Beverly Barton
Available July.

SNLHIBC

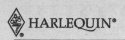

REQUEST YOUR FREE BOOKS!

2 FREE NOVELS PLUS 2 FREE GIFTS!

There's the life you planned. And there's what comes next.

NEXT07R

LIKE MOTHER, LIKE DAUGHTER
(But In a Good Way)

with stories by
Jennifer Greene,
Nancy Robards Thompson
and Peggy Webb

Don't miss these three unforgettable stories about the unbreakable—and sometimes infuriating—bonds between mothers and daughters and the men who get caught in the madness (when they're not causing it!).

HARLEQUIN®
Next™

Available May 2007
TheNextNovel.com

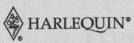

HARLEQUIN®

COMING NEXT MONTH

#83 LAST NIGHT AT THE HALFMOON •
Kate Austin

When Aimee King learns that the Halfmoon Drive-In is closing, it feels like the end of the world to her. Sure she loves her life: her son, her job, her parents who live down the street, even her ex-husband. But with the closing, she's about to learn there's something more important uniting all the people in her life....

#84 LIKE MOTHER, LIKE DAUGHTER
(BUT IN A GOOD WAY) • Jennifer Greene,
Nancy Robards Thompson and Peggy Webb

Don't miss these three unforgettable stories about the unbreakable—and sometimes infuriating—bonds between mothers and daughters and the men who get caught in the madness (when they're not causing it!).